DAX HARRISON

AN EXCITING NEW
SPACE ADVENTURE BY

TONY VALDEZ

This is a work of fiction. Names, characters, organizations, places, events, and incidents are either products of the author's imagination or are used fictitiously.

Dax Harrison was written before a live studio audience. . . . Just kidding. We use canned laughter.

Published by Inkshares, Inc., San Francisco, California
www.inkshares.com

Edited and designed by Story Perfect Editing Services and Reedsy
http://www.storyperfectediting.com/
https://reedsy.com/

Artwork by Jessica R. Van Hulle | Titles & cover design by Seth Kinkaid
Layouts by Kevin G. Summers

ISBN: 9781942645986
e-ISBN: 9781942645993
Library of Congress Control Number: 2017956950

First edition

Printed in the United States of America

This book is dedicated to all my friends and family who have put up with my endless babbling about wanting to tell stories. . . .

PROLOGUE

A LONE RINGED planet lies ahead as the United Territories Frigate *Alexandra* moves across the otherwise vast emptiness of space. Captain Charles Anders stands front and center on the bridge, politely sipping tea and admiring the view. He stands proudly, full of age and wisdom, as technicians, navigators, and the like shuffle about.

He turns to a young officer at a nearby console. "Surveillance, report."

"The sector is secure, Captain," Ensign Briggs replies. "No signs of enemy activity in the area."

"Very good. Keep her steady on. We'll make a quick pass around the planet and move out." Anders takes a look around. The long war has left his crew weary, and he can't afford mistakes. "Look alive, people. This is our last run in this quadrant. After this, we're headed back for some well-earned rack time." The crew responds with scattered smiles, cheers, and claps. Hope returns to their eyes.

Another young officer approaches, dapper and enthusiastic. "The Alliance will be happy to hear the Carteagans haven't made it past Feron, sir."

"Not on our watch, Lieutenant Harrison." The captain smiles back at his favorite bridge officer. "Takes us home, Dax."

Lieutenant Dax Harrison cheerfully salutes back. "Yes, sir!" With a boyish face, hopeful eyes, pristine uniform, and impeccable crew cut to match, the young man is the very embodiment of the optimistic spirit the Alliance stands for. As he moves back toward his navigation post, however . . .

BEEP, BEEP, BEEP, BEEP! An alert blares from the surveillance console. "Captain!" Briggs shouts. "We have incoming on our six!"

"Shields up!" Anders wastes no time.

"Stealth-class warbird, sir," Briggs continues. "It's the Carteagans!" Outside, a Carteagan stealth fighter de-cloaks and zooms down toward the *Alexandra*, twin laser cannons firing.

Anders barks orders at the crew as they scramble about the bridge. All business now. "Red alert! All hands to battle stations!"

"Captain! We've got incoming pulse blasts—"

BOOM! The strike cuts Briggs off as the ship rumbles and lurches. Scattered systems spark and short out, and several of the crew tumble to the deck.

The enemy fighter continues its assault. The craft is small, but the damage wrought by its blasts is calculated. It makes another pass, and the *Alexandra* takes another beating. More crew are sent flying. More sparks erupt from the once-pristine equipment. Anders holds himself up against a console. "Return fire, dammit!"

Tactical Officer Reynolds taps frantically at her screens. "Weapon systems offline, Captain!"

"Unacceptable! Get them back up, Ensign!"

"Trying, sir!"

In the cockpit of the stealth fighter, a vile grin stretches across the Carteagan pilot's face. A large humanoid alien, green with scales. Seemingly a combination of man, lizard, insect, and rage.

A third large blast rattles the ship. The console that Anders has been steadying himself with begins sparking and overloading.

"Captain!" Harrison dives, pushing Anders out of the way in the nick of time. The computer explodes in spark and flame. Pulling themselves from the floor, the two men freeze, eyes locked on the main viewscreen as a massive Carteagan warship de-cloaks in space ahead.

The assault ceases for a moment as a voice takes over the ship's intercoms.

"Alliance vessel, shut down your engines and prepare to be boarded. Comply, or you will be destroyed." Anders gets back to his feet, grimacing at the Carteagan commander's ultimatum.

"We've got to run for it."

Harrison is shocked at his captain. "Sir, shouldn't we stand and fight?"

"We're out of options, Harrison." Another strike. Reynolds goes down for the count. Harrison takes command of the tactical station.

"Sir, the hyperdrive is fried. On regular engines, they'll run us down in minutes."

Anders lowers his head in exasperation. "Do you have any better suggestions?"

The lieutenant gazes out to the view of the nearby planet, an idea sparking behind his eyes. "Head for Feron."

"What?"

"Let them chase us into the planet's ring. We put all power to the rear shields, but leave the deflectors down. We'll need to hold out just long enough."

"For *what*, Harrison?"

He turns to Anders with a grin. "The right moment, sir."

Moments later, the *Alexandra* moves toward the ring, passing through a sea of dust and rock. The Carteagan warship follows. The enemy commander returns to the intercom. "You think you can hide? Ha! Foolish humans! You will be destroyed, along with the rest of your pitiful race! This galaxy is ours!"

Another blast sends the pilot flying from his seat. Harrison takes the helm.

"Shields at twenty percent," Anders warns. "The time is now!"

"Activating tractor!" Harrison's hands fly across the console controls with precision. In space, a tractor beam activates in a column of light behind the *Alexandra*. Slowly, it begins to pull a large asteroid toward the ship, towing it close behind. Meanwhile, the warship continues pursuit, closing in fast.

From the bridge of the warship, the Carteagan commander glares at the *Alexandra*, narrowing his gaze at the asteroid in tow.

Harrison monitors the action from the helm. Their dreaded pursuers are directly behind them now. Anders prepares himself at a nearby console.

"Ready?"

"Ready!"

"Deflectors on in three, two, one!" Both men slam down on their controls in unison. Outside, a storm of light begins to build at the rear of the ship. A fiery orange force field grows rapidly as the deflector energy smashes against the tractor beam. The two opposing forces rumble the entire ship, threatening to tear it to pieces.

Tension mounts for a moment as Anders and Harrison watch from the bridge monitors, beads of sweat at their temples. More systems malfunction under the strain, overloading and bursting into flames. Anders shields himself from flying sparks.

"Now, Dax! Now!" Harrison slams the controls again, releasing the tractor beam. The stifled deflector energy erupts, rocketing the massive asteroid back toward the pursuing warship. There's no time to react. Rock and ship collide, and the Carteagans are obliterated in a spectacular crash.

Harrison breathes a sigh of relief. Roots and cheers are heard throughout the bridge from whatever crew members remain conscious. Hugs, pats on the back, and the like. Anders turns to Harrison with a salute.

"That was damn fine work, Lieutenant. I bet those green bastards will think twice after losing one of their flagships."

"Thank you, sir." He returns the salute.

"I may be exceeding my authority here, but I'd say the Alliance owes you a promotion when we get back." Before Harrison can respond, an explosion is heard from the entry to the bridge. All eyes lock on as the door slides open. The stealth fighter pilot barges in with a hostage in his grip. The young lady cadet shouts in protest as the Carteagan barbarically shoves her into the room, a disintegration pistol trained to her head.

"Who destroyed the *Akshaata*?" The reptilian alien hisses with fury. Harrison isn't fazed. He approaches his enemy, boldly standing mere steps away, face-to-face.

"I did. Just as I'll destroy you, unless you let her go."

The creature growls in return. "You shall all pay for this . . . in your blood!"

The lady cadet stuns the Carteagan with an elbow to the jaw. Harrison lunges at the Carteagan, pushing the pistol away. It fires, missing the young woman by inches. They struggle for control a moment, but Harrison deftly performs a series of Krav Maga hand and elbow strikes, stunning the attacking alien. The gun drops free, and in one swift motion, Harrison grabs the free-falling pistol, spins around, blasts the Carteagan into dust, and catches the falling cadet in his arms.

She gazes into her hero's eyes. "You . . . you saved me."

"Those were some smart moves yourself, Cadet."

"He almost had me there for a second," she continues, holding tightly to Harrison's rippling muscles.

He smiles back. "Not on my watch, Miss—?"

"Calico, Cassie Calico. And you are?"

"Dax Harrison, at your service." The two kiss passionately, Miss Calico still dipped in his arms, her long golden hair blowing in a wind that seems to come from nowhere. The rest of the crew explodes with applause and cheers all around. The music swells and . . .

The scene continued on the television as a young ten-year-old boy watched on, gleefully awestruck. He gripped tightly to his Commander Harrison action figure, palms sweaty from the excitement of the made-for-TV movie.

"Alex," his mother lovingly but impatiently called. "Dinner's getting cold on the table!"

"Okay!" Begrudgingly, he set the toy down, climbed off his Commander Harrison bedsheets, and headed out to the hallway as the commercial announcements began.

"Our feature presentation of *Commander Harrison: Birth of a Legend* will continue after these brief messages. . . ."

CHAPTER 1

DAX (THE REAL Dax) sat drunkenly snoring up a storm, dead to the world. He had propped his boots up on the control console in front of him and reclined the pilot's seat as far back as possible. It wasn't nearly as cozy as his bunk, but it was serviceable enough when he was too drunk to bother stumbling to the far end of the ship. This also created the perfect angle for cradling a liquor bottle at crotch level. Perfect, that is, until the ship began to rock, sending it flying to the floor.

The continued turbulence woke Dax to the fruits of his labor.

"Ugh. Son of a biiiitch," he moaned, attempting to rub the hangover away through his temples. He gazed over to the bottle on the floor. *Cheap-ass Verdasian wine,* he thought. *Never again.* The ship lurched some more, and Dax sat up, steadying himself. *What now?* A flashing red light on the console caught his eye.

"SAMM?" He turned to his side, expecting an answer. Nothing. The protracted mechanical cylinder, branded "SAMM" along its side, hung lifeless from the ceiling. Annoyed, he focused his eyes back on the blinking alert. The distant rumbling from outside was growing to an unnerving roar now. A few quick taps on the console and the cockpit shutters began to open. Instantly, an incredible light flooded the ship, blinding Dax. The nose of the *Crichton* glowed hot orange and white, burning up from the steep, high-speed entry into the atmosphere.

The legendary Commander Dax Harrison was crashing into a planet.

"What the fu—AHH!" The ship rocked again, knocking him out of his seat. Scrambling back up, he yanked hard on the yoke to little avail. "SAMM, where the hell are you?" He tapped frantically at the console, searching for the SAMM restart. "Need a little help here! Wake up!" A few more taps and the lifeless cylinder lit up with a holographic display surrounding it.

"Commander," the artificial voice replied cheerfully.

"Hi there," Dax replied just as cheerfully. "HELP, YOU IDIOT!" Immediately, SAMM's systems kicked into gear, assuming control and leveling the descent. In the seconds it took to do this, however, Dax braced for impact, scrambled to think of a god to pray to, and quite possibly peed a drop or two.

"We are now approaching our destination within acceptable speeds and vector, Commander."

Dax slumped back into his chair, catching his breath and wiping a bit of panic sweat from his brow. "What the hell was that?"

"The M-class planet Saleon. Also known as Celestial Body—"

"Yeah, I know it's a planet. Why the hell were we crashing into it? What happened to the autopilot?"

Ever the efficient AI, SAMM was already searching the logs. "System records show autopilot function was disabled two hours, thirty-six minutes ago from the primary command console."

Dax glanced at his boots, then over at the console, ashamedly making sense of it.

"I would have corrected our course," SAMM continued. "However, that was approximately one hour after you shut down *my* systems as well, stating that I was 'killing your buzz.'"

Dax rubbed his temples, the explanation amplifying his hangover. "All right, all right, fine. Just get us on the ground."

"Commander, due to our increased speed, we are approximately one hour early. Might I recommend a shower and perhaps a shave?"

They just had *to give him a personality,* Dax thought. "What are you trying to say, Sammy? I'm not pretty enough for a cargo run?"

"I simply would imagine your adoring fans may expect someone a bit more . . . presentable."

Dax looked over to a small mirror on the wall, double-taking as he realized SAMM might have a point. Dark circles had invaded the real estate around his lower eyelids. His hair matched the level of chaos in his alcohol-rattled guts. And if he was being very honest with himself, he wasn't entirely sure if it had been two or three days since he'd changed shirts. *Oh, there's the ketchup stain from the eggs. Three days.*

He sighed heavily, mentally preparing for the oncoming routine. With much grumbling, he headed back toward the ship corridor. "Right. Just land us at the station. I'll be out, eventually."

The SSV *Crichton* soared across the lush, natural landscape of Saleon. Crystal-blue waters and expansive forest lands stretched far into the distance, breaking only for the equally stunning snowcapped mountains on the horizon. The only smudge in the postcard-like view was the *Crichton* itself. The small cargo vessel had seen better days. Better decades, actually. But the Alliance didn't necessarily dole out the fresh paint jobs and replacement parts for an old hauler like this. Such was the trade-off if you wanted to coast your way into retirement, and Dax was perfectly content staying off the Alliance's radar until then.

The viewscreen in Dax's bunk intercepted an auto-play transmission. He tuned in and out, half-listening to the narrator as he continued shaving.

"With four major settlements, the planet Saleon is home to both booming industry and magnificent natural beauty." He peeked over and caught a glimpse of the images designed to capture tourist wallets. *Hmm, not bad.* Dax had business here, but this was the first time he'd had the opportunity to visit himself. Maybe this cargo run wouldn't be so boring after all. Turning to a marker board on the wall, he jotted down Saleon under an ongoing list of possible retirement locales.

Minutes later, SAMM landed the *Crichton* at Saleon Outpost One, and Dax was immediately met with a small group of officers in the hangar bay. Leading the pack was a young deck officer, attempting and failing to hold back his enthusiasm.

"Commander Harrison, welcome!" The greeting was awkwardly loud and accompanied by a salute so vigorous, Dax thought he might have bruised his forehead. *Oh, great. A superfan.* Nevertheless, Dax switched on the commanding charm.

"At ease, Officer. . . ?"

"Merris," he continued. "And, Commander, if I may say so, it is an honor to have you here at Saleon One."

"Well, it is my pleasure to personally see these goods delivered to one of the finest colonies in all of the United

Territories." Dax maintained a smile through gritted teeth, as Merris glowed at his idol's acknowledgment.

"Please, right the way, sir." He signaled the other men to attend to unloading the supplies, while he and Dax made their way off the platform.

Dax took in the gorgeous surroundings of the main promenade. The settlement was a giant tourist-trap resort. Where there wasn't a hotel, restaurant, or other luxury business, there was a viewscreen advertising one. Dax also noted an expansive tech boutique along the way. He tapped the communication pin on his uniform.

"Hey, Sammy, tell me again about those servo upgrades you were looking at."

"Well, the 9700 series is quite exquisite but currently overpriced due to demand. The 9450 line, while not as efficient, would be a suitably budgeted improvement."

"The 97s it is."

"You're a wonderful man!" SAMM shouted. "I mean, thank you, Commander."

Dax smirked. "Don't say I never did anything for you." Dax's reputation proceeded him as he and Merris made their way. Onlookers whispered at his passing and gazed at the legendary hero. Dax returned with nods, smiles, and glances back, paying special attention to some of the more beautiful women passing by. What a ham.

"As you can see, Commander," Merris continued. "We are the largest and most popular of the Saleon colonies—"

"Uh-huh," Dax replied occasionally, feigning interest as Merris rattled on.

"Business really has boomed in the last year, and with your endorsement for the new resort, which again I thank you immensely for so graciously agreeing to, we can expect a doubling if not tripling of our previous margin."

Dax stopped in front of a gorgeous water fountain at the center of the promenade. He always did appreciate faux Greek statues and their proclivity for topless marble women. "Say, listen, how long is this deal gonna take? Not to rush things. I've just got a lot of important stuff to take care of during my stay," he said as he decided which casino to visit first.

"Oh, absolutely, Commander. We'll have you in and out of the studio in no time flat!"

Moments later, Dax was barging into the foyer of Zellev's, the most popular, most lavish resort on the colony. Instantly, a crowd of rabid fans swarmed from the ground-floor casino. Screaming ladies, photographers, a gentleman offering a tropical drink with an umbrella in it, and so on.

"Thank you!" Dax gushed. "Thank you, everybody!" He slowly made his way through the sea of people, shaking hands and smiling for the cameras as Merris fell behind.

"If we can make our way, Commander!" Merris shouted over the cacophony. "We'll need you on Level Three in about twenty minutes."

Dax sipped his complimentary drink. "You know, Dennis, I think I might actually take some time and have a look around. There's no rush, is there?"

"Merris!" he politely corrected. "Um, not at all, Commander! I'll have the crew standing by at your convenience."

"Terrific. Appreciate it, Dennis." Dax carried on with the crowd, signing autographs and schmoozing.

CHAPTER 2

SR822 WAS A garbage heap of a planet at the ass end of the Territories, but it had its uses. Chiefly, being a garbage heap. The Darshyll originally used the barren landscape as a literal landfill for anything too costly or otherwise unfeasible for recycling. For decades, everything from scavenged ship remains to discarded children's toys formed majestic mountain ranges of waste. In an ironic twist, valuable deposits of iridium were eventually discovered beneath the surface, and thus the Pit was born.

The worst of the worst lived out their days here. Some of the most vicious maniacs, serial killers, and all-purpose scum of the universe were shipped in to mine the precious ore until their bodies gave out. This was the end of the road. No escape. No release, save for death. And for a former proud warrior, who once fought for the glory of his people in the greatest army the galaxy had ever seen, it was nearly enough to break him. Nearly.

Khern swung his pickax into the rock wall. Like the rest of the prisoners down the line, he stared ahead in a trance-like haze. This was life now, as it would be until age or a hidden blade would take him. Part of him welcomed it. And yet he pressed on. A fool's hope. Carteagan pride, perhaps. No, a promise.

A nearby prisoner fell to his knees, worked to the bone. Seconds later, he was met with an electrified stun baton to the back. It was a routine affair, but it was enough to pull Khern out of his daze. He grimaced at the Darshyll guard delivering the punishment. The race was commonly described not unlike the warthogs of Earth. Hairy, odious, disagreeable. The tusks and snout did them no favors either, leading to quite the awkward conversations upon first contact with humanity. They made fast allies, however, integrating and improving Earth's resources and marking the beginnings of the Alliance.

Slurs against Carteagans, on the other hand, were generally more acceptable, especially in circles still harboring deep resentment from the war. "Croc-bug" or "croc-hopper," crossing crocodiles with grasshoppers, were the most popular terms. Humans. So quick to judge, categorize, and catalog the universe how they see fit. When Khern arrived in the Pit, he made fast work of the first inmate to irritate his ears with such insults. Removing his tongue was quite the effective display, ensuring peace and quiet for the rest of his stay. It also ensured a swift and vicious beating from the guards, but he still felt it was well worth it.

In the long run, grudges didn't serve much purpose in a colony of lifers. So when a giant Darshyll guard by the name of Ertac deliberately bumped into him, knocking Khern to the ground and telling him to get back to work, he didn't retaliate. Instead, Khern picked up his ax and covertly pocketed the small item the guard had slipped in his hand during the commotion.

He wouldn't get a good look at it until the end of the workday. Like clockwork, the prisoners filed into their sleeping quarters. There was never much disobedience or rabble-rousing at lights-out. Even the younger inmates, still obliged to prove their toughness at every opportunity, were broken by the time they were allowed to put down their tools.

As Ertac and the rest of the guards left the area, Khern examined the gift. A small rectangular stick of metal. A holo-cell. This is what they had been waiting for. At least, that's what he hoped. The reason he kept his promise. The reason Khern chose not to give in to the Pit. Quietly, he made his way toward the far end of the sleeping quarters, past rows of other prisoners with either curiosity or annoyance on their faces. Finally, he arrived at his destination, taking great care not to disturb the occupant.

"General, forgive my intrusion." He spoke softly but with intent. "The contact has delivered."

Eyldwan Utynai. He said nothing for a moment, remaining seated in a meditative position against the back wall. Finally, he opened his eyes, examining the holo-cell Khern had extended to him. He took it and swiped his finger across its edge, activating it. A holographic display projected from the device, glowing between the two prisoners. Khern observed Eyldwan's face before him, now lit up from the projection. A fellow Carteagan, aged in years and experience. A sizeable and intimidating scar of some previous battle traced the right side of the general's jaw. Khern watched as the jaw gave way to menacing teeth.

A sinister grin developed as the eyes above it scanned the holographic data. Schematics of some kind. A large cylindrical object. An oversized missile, perhaps. Further schematics cycled through the air between them, detailing a facility of some sort.

"Ready the men. We leave tonight."

CHAPTER 3

"COME ON, YOU piece of crap." Dax fiddled with the lapel microphone, which refused to stay clipped to his shirt. He struggled for an inordinate amount of time as he allowed himself to be distracted by the long legs of his interviewer.

Marisa Chambers, renowned journalist, had sat down with presidents, diplomats, and the first pro human/Darshyll football team. She had previously asked the commander for an interview spot, but he held out after she had bamboozled an A-list actor, in what he thought would be a fluff piece, with a series of hard-hitting questions on camera about his extramarital affairs and accusations of tax evasion. This, however, she assured Dax, would be a lighthearted chat about his upcoming retirement plans. No more, no less. After a brief and flirtatious phone call, and a quick look at his tax records, Dax agreed.

"Dax Harrison," she began as the cameras rolled. "Lieutenant commander in the Allied Forces of the United Territories Alliance. A celebrated war hero, whose exploits throughout the years have become the subject of several biographical books, docudramas, and film adaptations."

Dax sat nodding and smiling as she listed his accomplishments. "Oh, you mean me!" he jokingly exclaimed with fake surprise.

Marisa laughed in return with fake amusement. "Commander, you are now nearing the end of your service, and you have received some criticism in the public eye regarding your post-retirement plans. In particular, your decision to partner with several businesses in the hotel and gambling industries, some right here on Saleon." Marisa's warm, charming smile began to fade. "Some of which have even faced previous accusations of questionable practices."

Crap. Dax squirmed in his seat a little. "That, that seems a bit blown out of proportion—"

"Many citizens see this as a highly controversial move from a public figure such as yourself." She continued without letting him finish.

"Now, I hardly think that—"

"We have a viewer submission here from a teacher, mother of two on Earth, in Iowa." Marisa held her personal tablet in view of the camera before reading from it. "'Commander, I appreciate all you have done for the Alliance, but how can I have my sons looking up to a role model who smiles for the camera while profiting with gangsters and back-alley thugs?'"

"Gangsters and thugs?" Dax chuckled nervously. "Okay, this is clearly a whole bunch of misunderstanding." He kept smiling, but he knew what this was. She did it. She conned him for ratings, and he was stupid enough to fall for it. Who knew if what she said was true? Dax had endorsement deals all over the place. How was he to know if a few business partners happened to have some shady dealings?

"Well, Commander?" Marisa waited for an answer, eyes locked to his like missiles.

My God, is she even blinking? He thought for a moment. Fortunately, Dax had years of experience at his disposal in one of the most crucial, tactical skill sets for a man in his position: lying through his damned teeth.

"Miss Chambers. I'm sorry, Marisa, is it? I'm going to go out on a limb and say you seem to have me pegged as a man who's trying to get away with something. Now, I'll be straight with you. Despite what you may believe, judging by the look on your face, I take my business associations seriously, and I take the good people of the Territories seriously."

"That is good to hear, Commander."

"So if any of those associates were to be called on the carpet for some kind of dishonorable or unethical behaviors, I assure you, I would see to it personally that justice be done." He poised with the expertise of someone running for office, complete with a pointed finger.

"I think the people of the Alliance would expect nothing less." She smiled politely back, which Dax read as, "Touché."

"Did your sources happen to mention that all my arrangements include a large portion of the proceeds going to charity? Because that's true, you know." He lowered his head in faux humbleness. "I don't like to flaunt it, but since we're digging here, maybe I could share a bit on why I came to that decision."

"Please do, Commander." Marisa signaled the cameraman to cut to a close-up.

Dax knew the angle. She was trying to keep him in the hot seat, but this was where he shone. "A few years back I was on Titan, the Galant colony. As I'm sure you know, the damage from the war left that place wide-open to mercenaries, war criminals, back-alley thugs, as you put it. They scavenged the leftovers after the Carteagan bombings, and Galant was hit the hardest." He sighed heavily, playing up the uneasiness evoked by the memory. "I can't tell you how long those final skirmishes lasted, or how many bodies hit the dirt, but by the end of it, I felt like I just walked through hell."

Dax glanced at the cameraman and noticed his wide-eyed gaze. He went on. "An hour after the dust settled, my team and I were securing the area, checking what was left of the colony for survivors. I found an eight-year-old boy sitting in a burned-down shack and crying for his parents. They were dead in the next room. Executed by the mercs. We figured the boy had been there for a couple days like that. Days, Ms. Chambers." Dax looked away with a thousand-yard stare. "I carried him out of the wreckage and straight onto an evac shuttle. He asked me why bad things like that happen." He shook his head, eyes glazing over ever so slightly. "I didn't have an answer for him. I still don't."

Dax looked straight at Marisa, wiping away a stray tear. "My team and I, we were lucky, Ms. Chambers. We did the job and got to go home. Hell didn't come for us. Hell kicked down that kid's door. And that's what I think about when I offer my support to colonies like Saleon One. That child and others like him are the reason I do what I do. And you'll have to excuse me if I find them to be a worthwhile investment."

Dax looked around the room. Not a dry eye in sight. *Perfect.*

The next morning, Dax awoke to the chirping of his comms pin on the nightstand. A quick glance around the hotel suite and the previous evening came back to him through the fog. Dinner, drinks, a few blurry events after that. He reached over and tapped the pin, knocking over a half-empty champagne bottle in the process.

"Yeah?"

"Commander," SAMM replied. "You have an incoming communication."

"What the—I'm busy. Have 'em leave a message."

"It's Captain Sykes, Commander."

"Ah jeez. All right, all right. Just give me a second." Dax composed himself quickly, careful not to disturb Marisa, still sound asleep. He relocated to a desk at the far end of the luxury suite, grabbing his uniform shirt and jacket from the floor and dressing himself along the way. "Okay, send him through." He set the comms pin flat on the desk and adjusted his hair just in time as the holographic face of his former commanding officer projected above it.

"Commander Harrison."

"Captain! What a pleasant surprise!" The words came out a little too eager. Officially, Sykes was no longer Dax's direct superior, but he never failed to intimidate Dax with his occasional check-ins. In fact, he rather delighted in it. The captain was just shy of fifty and still as tough as nails, as far as Dax was concerned. The sight of his salt-and-peppery regulation haircut alone was enough to fill Dax with a sense of foreboding. A receding harbinger of doom.

"How are things on the outer rim?"

"Excellent, sir. Terrific. Just completing the supply drop at Saleon. Everything is business as usual—"

"Cut the shit, Harrison."

"Cutting it, sir."

"I've got an assignment I want to discuss with you in person. I'll need you at Central ASAP."

"Assignment, sir?"

"You're being reactivated for Special Tactics."

Dax's face dropped. "Sir, I was under the impression I was to be relieved in three months."

"Plans change, Harrison. Stop by Command after your delivery. You'll receive your full orders there. Sykes out."

The hologram disappeared abruptly, leaving Dax sitting alone and dumbfounded. He took a deep, calming breath.

"Well, shit."

CHAPTER 4

THE MASSIVE UNITED Central Space Station orbited Earth below. When humans first expanded into space, it was assumed the simple nuisances of terrestrial life would be a thing of the past, giving way to grander, more imperative issues at hand. It was a foolish assumption, as proven by the constant traffic jam of arriving and departing ships forever buzzing around the station. Serving as headquarters for the human arm of the Alliance Navy, along with both civilian and military spaceports, Dax wasn't alone in considering the aging station as a bloated, lumbering mess.

He made his way down the main public plaza toward the administrative offices. One perk of the station's constant bustling crowds was that Dax was easily able to blend in during most of his visits here.

"Commander!"

Most of his visits. Scattered whispers and shouts echoed through the plaza, and Dax responded with crowd-pleasing waves perfected with routine. Hard to complain when it paid the bills, yet he breathed an eye-rolling sigh of relief once out of sight. His personal phone buzzed in his pocket just as he entered a more secluded hallway.

"Harrison," he answered.

"Donating to charity?" The voice on the other end was clearly not happy.

"How ya doing, Eddie?"

"Are you outta your goddamned mind?!" Zellev's right-hand man and business manager, Eddie (last name unknown), wasn't much of a people person on a good day, let alone after watching Dax promise resort profits away on the air.

"I had to say something! I was being backed into a corner!" Dax looked around, making sure no one could hear his whispered shouts. "And what's this about questionable practices, huh? Is your boss running a mob out there or something? Is that new hotel sitting on a foundation of busted kneecaps?"

"I have no recollection of that, Your Honor." The line was rehearsed plenty. "Meantime, that charity of yours? It'll be coming out of your share only. Got it? A hundred percent!"

The call dropped before Dax could get a word in edgewise. *Gangsters and thugs,* he thought. *Okay, maybe Marisa had a point.* But it was nothing to worry about. Soon enough he'd be out of the service, and he still had other completely legitimate business arrangements to supplement his retirement. Such as the Japanese toothpaste company, a cardboard standee for which stood in the window of a gift shop directly in front of him at that very moment. Dax stared at the cartoon image of himself, beaming back at him with comically oversized eyes and sparkling teeth.

"They never get my eyes right."

"Do you know what the current public opinion is of the Alliance Navy, Lieutenant Weaver?"

Logan stood at attention near the doorway of Sykes's office, contemplating how best to answer the question. Ever the soldier, she went with the response drilled into her head since her academy days. "Sir, we are the proud and diligent protectors of our—"

Sykes dropped his SmartNews paper onto his desk with a disapproving thud, the damning headlines glitching for a moment before continuing to scroll. "You can cut the good soldier routine with me, Lieutenant. I'm not talking about those bullshit public service announcements."

"Right, sir. Sorry, sir."

"And sit down, would you? You're making me nervous."

She did so. There was a warmth between them of old friends, despite the age gap. Having grown up on the station, some of the career officers were more familiar than family at times. Now in her late twenties, she remained acutely aware of her demeanor, and dared not chance any excuse for her fellow officers to claim favoritism. Her title was the sole product of her work, her skill, her blood, and her sweat.

Sykes, on the other hand, was seasoned enough to not care in the slightest for mincing words. "The people don't care about us anymore. More than that, they want us gone. Recruitment is at an all-time low, and the only time we see any press is when some jackass politician convinces everyone that we're the boogeyman behind their tax hikes."

Logan stifled a chuckle. "With all due respect, sir, I never imagined you to be much for politics."

"One of the unfortunate responsibilities of promotion," he said, resigned. "And in the hope of turning this tide, the top brass are launching a bit of a campaign. There's going to be a lot of PR, some new recruitment spots. The tenth anniversary of the cease-fire will make a good opportunity for a public song and dance."

Logan nodded along, still unclear what a PR campaign had to do with her. Sykes appeared particularly perturbed as he shared the next detail.

"We're bringing in Dax Harrison."

"Commander Harrison?" *THE Commander Harrison?* she thought.

"You're familiar with him, I take it?"

"Of course. Well, I mean, not personally, but everyone knows Commander Harrison."

"Uh-huh. What do you know about him?"

Logan stared quizzically at him for a moment, trying to decipher the necessity for such a grammar school lesson. "He's a decorated officer. Led the *Alexandra* into battle at Feron. Destroyed the Carteagans' largest warship by turning an asteroid into a projectile. Records now refer to it as the Harrison Maneuver. Went on to command—"

Sykes held his hand up. "All right, that's enough. Hero of the Alliance, right?" He reached into his desk drawer, produced a small paperback novel, and tossed it to her. "You ever read that crap? Personally, I think they make me sound like an asshole."

Logan examined the cover, an atrociously cheesy artwork featuring an idealized version of Dax front and center. Rippling muscles, damsel in one arm, laser rifle in the other. "Permission to speak freely, sir?"

"Of course."

"While I admire the commander's service record, I find it very odd that Command has allowed an active-duty officer to profit from his exploits."

"Harrison has been allowed some special privileges, but we make sure nothing classified gets out. And after the war, well, the people needed a hero."

That much was true. Logan had a front-row seat to the flood of refugees that poured into Central during the war. At sixteen, she was just shy of academy age by the cease-fire, but she had unofficially helped run supplies between the station's medical wards during the worst of it. Humanity's back was near broken. And were it not for the victory at Feron, the final straw may have snapped it.

"Regardless how much history gets embellished," Sykes continued, "Harrison is the face they trust. So, he'll be overseeing the campaign, and I want you as his second-in-command."

Logan had been enjoying a long stint on the SSV *Combine*, Admiral Bennett's frigate, where she had hoped to stay. Working with the commander, however, could be quite the opportunity. "Sir, I don't know what to say. It's an honor, but I'm no public relations officer."

"No, no. Harrison will handle all that. I just want you to keep an eye on him for me. Assist in any way you can, and make sure he stays . . . on point." Sykes seemed to be choosing his words carefully, which was not his usual modus operandi. But Logan knew he wasn't one for playing games. If he wanted her on an op, it was for a good reason.

"Tell me where to report, sir. I'll be there."

"Good. I'll keep you posted. I knew I could count on you, Weaver." He stood to show her to the door. "You know, some of us still feel the hole your father left in this station. I'm sure he'd be proud to see you filling it in his stead."

"Thank you, sir." The compliment ran deep. So much so that she almost forgot the nagging question at the back of her mind. "Sir? How much of that history you mentioned is embellished?"

"That's classified, Lieutenant." He shut the door on her.

CHAPTER 5

"I CAN'T DO it."

"Yes, you can."

Dax slowly opened his eyes, huffing and puffing for his life. He was exhausted. Every muscle ached. Sweat dripped down his face, and the world was a spinning blur. "I've got nothing left."

"Dig deep. You've got this."

The back of his head stung and throbbed. He grasped at it and felt a warm wetness. Blood was on his fingers. "I'm done for. Just leave me to die."

"All right, sir, now you're being overdramatic," SAMM protested through the comms pin.

Dax lumbered slowly to his feet, shooting a stink eye to the treadmill that bested him, and the wall that broke his fall. "Easy for you to say. Titanium alloy doesn't get a beer gut. Hell, you don't even rust."

"Technically speaking, it is possible but at an extremely slow rate. I suspect you would be long gone before that becomes a problem."

Dax stopped the treadmill and headed toward the locker room. "Oh, don't talk like that Sammy. You and me, we're gonna live forever." He said it confidently, though he had been noticing more and more gray hairs around his temples as of late. And the extra lines on his brow. And the absurd way he pulled a muscle by simply reaching for an engine coil that came loose a week ago. His thirties were halfway over, and it was becoming clearer that he was going to have to either shape up quick or resign himself to the fact that hard living was going to keep catching up.

"Unless perhaps, both our lifespans are cut short by extenuating circumstances," SAMM replied. "Say, a crash landing?"

"You're really not letting that one go, are you?" Dax sighed as he stood at the locker room sinks, rinsing the spot of blood from the back of his head. "Come on. I bought you your fancy servos, didn't I?"

"And I am graciously thanking you by keeping you on track. Ten more minutes of cardio, then the barbell."

Dax groaned, throwing a towel over his head and reluctantly marching back. He would spend the next month docked at Central, rotating through the station's multiple expansive fitness centers. Dax had never struggled with any significant weight issues per se, but as Sykes put it, "Get back in fighting shape. The people need to see their hero, and what you got there isn't exactly muscle, is it?" A training montage, like the ones from his movies, would have been convenient right about now.

He appreciated it finally as he was buttoning up his dress uniform with ease, on the way to the cease-fire anniversary opening gala. He stood in the lift, mumbling to himself. "On behalf of the Alliance, we welcome Ambassador Ni—Nilana. Ni . . . hama. Dammit." He gave up and tapped his comms pin.

"Harrison to Sykes."

The massive grand hall was filled with Alliance military, high society attendees, and press for the extravagant gala. Sykes stood in a greeting line by the entrance, exchanging handshakes, salutes, and smiles with the entering dignitaries as his comms pin chimed.

"Hey, Cap. You there?"

"Dax, where the hell are you?"

"On the way." Dax admired the fit of his old uniform, flexing to the reflective wall of the lift. "What's that Carteagan ambassador's name again? Nilana? Nirana Banana?"

Sykes rolled his eyes. "Ni-dah-nah. And you'd better get it right. They take pride in the family names. Now get here quick. The admiral wants us smiling for the cameras, and if I'm suffering through it, so are you."

"Got it." The lift stopped and the doors slid open. Dax readied his charmer smile and walked out into the grand hall. He took in his surroundings. To his left, Sykes and the dignitaries. To his front, the grand ballroom floor, with a stage and podium behind it. His smile faded slightly, as he bet himself ten credits they would make him give a speech tonight. To his right, *Ah-ha! The bar!*

He made it two steps before a hand on his shoulder stopped him in his tracks.

"Commander Harrison!" Dax turned to see Admiral Bennett. The man was nearing his midsixties, but his iron grip kept firm on Dax, juxtaposed with a warm smile.

"Admiral. Reporting for duty, sir."

"Oh, nonsense. It's a party, Harrison. Relax."

"Thank you, sir." The two expert bullshitters, well aware of their mutual dislike for each other, carried on with their smiles. Bennett released his grip, leading Dax toward Sykes and the dignitaries.

"It's been a while since you've been back here at Central, hasn't it?" Bennett continued. "I trust you found your way to the party all right?" Dax heard the translation in his head. *Why the hell are you late?*

"Yes, sir. No trouble at all."

"Glad to hear it. Nidahna!" Much to Dax's relief, the admiral turned his attention to Ambassador Nidahna. The female Carteagan was sure to turn more than a few heads at the party. Middle-aged (which was around the 150s for her species), she wore an elegant gown and was pulling it off in spades. Despite the green pigment and scales, even Dax had to admit she was rather stunning. He briefly wondered whether that was meant as a cunning negotiation tactic.

"Ambassador, this is Commander Dax Harrison," Bennett announced.

"Commander." Nidahna greeted him with a subtle bow.

"Ambassador." Dax returned the gesture.

"Admiral Bennett, always a pleasure."

"Oh, Nidahna. Xavier, please." The ambassador and the admiral exchanged pleasantries for a few moments as Dax smiled politely, keeping his amusement to himself. *Lousy poker faces, these two.* Half a minute of small talk, and Dax knew that giving him grief was the only other thing in the world to give Bennett such joy.

"And it is a pleasure to finally meet you, Commander," she continued. "I have heard a great many things."

"Oh. Well, I hope you won't hold that against me." Small, polite laughs all around.

At that moment, a nearby buffet table was incurring the wrath of a hungry young corporal, saved only as he overheard the laughs and looked up. His eyes widened across his boyish face as he spotted Dax in the crowd.

"Commander Harrison," he announced to himself in awe. For a moment, the world around him began to quiet. Nothing else in the room mattered as *the* Commander Dax Harrison stood a mere twenty feet away.

"Sanders . . ."

The young man remained, seemingly catatonic as chunks of au gratin potato slid from his spoon and plopped back to the serving dish.

"Sanders!" Med Chief Dan O'Reilly smacked Sanders on the arm, knocking him out of his trance. "Jesus, kid. Come on, you're holding up the line." The two moved down the table, Sanders still fixated on Dax and O'Reilly grumbling over the lack of finger food selection.

"Now if you'll excuse me, gentlemen," Nidahna concluded, "I have a salad bar to raid."

More polite laughs. Bennett extended his elbow. "I'll join you." She took it, and they walked off, leaving Dax to annoy Sykes.

"He seems . . . uncharacteristically charming tonight, wouldn't you say?"

"Don't start."

Dax refrained, but he could only resist for a moment. "I guess some like it green, huh?"

"Shut up, Harrison." Sykes walked off. Dax followed shortly behind.

"Do Carteagans blush? I honestly don't know. I'm amazed Bennett can, that's for sure. . . ."

The rest of the evening flashed by in a blur, or dragged in a slow slog depending on whose opinion was asked. Dax posed with smiles and charm through some photo ops, shaking hands with Bennett and standing alongside Nidahna and other Alliance delegates. Later, the admiral would pull Sykes aside for a private chat, in which he requested Sykes's reassurance that Dax wouldn't muck up the campaign.

"There's been talk, Captain," Bennett warned. "And the public is catching wind. Harrison's outlived his usefulness, as far as I'm concerned, but if he wants to keep his retirement package, he'd better see this through."

"If I'm sure of anything, sir, it's Dax's sense of self-preservation," Sykes reassured himself as well as the admiral.

"Fine. So long as he doesn't screw up, he can have his honorary and be out of our hair for good. I'm tired of that wiseass."

As expected, Dax found himself pushed to the podium before the night was through. With the help of some prepared cards, he thanked the gala attendees, congratulated Nidahna and the other Alliance ambassadors for maintaining diplomacy in the galactic community, and recounted a brief but harrowing encounter during the final days of the war.

"And when I saw their leader," Dax carried on in full bravado, "in the middle of that battlefield, death surrounding us, I looked him dead in the eye—" He paused briefly, glancing at the note cards on the podium. "I looked him dead in the eye and said, 'Earth? Surrender? Not on my watch!'"

Applause ran through the grand hall, Sanders markedly jumping the gun near the back of the crowd. Dax silently wondered how he still managed to make that terrible line sell. He figured the thanks was owed to Chet Fontana, the long-running star of several Commander Harrison cinematic adventures. *That handsome jerk is better at playing me than me,* Dax mused.

The night wore on, and he was eventually allowed to wander off to exactly where he planned to be in the first place. Sanders spotted Dax nursing a drink at the bar, daydreaming into it. He approached, hardly containing his glee.

"Commander?" Dax remained in his daze. "Um, Commander, sir? Sorry to disturb you. I just wanted to say that was a great speech earlier. The Battle of Tarsis Three was always my favorite story from the war."

Dax poured himself a refill while Sanders rattled on. He wasn't in the mood, but he made a halfhearted attempt at feigning interest. "Oh, why thank you—"

"Sanders. Alex Sanders, sir. I really enjoyed the movie, too, but I wish they'd captured more of your dealings with the Darshyll mercenaries after the battle."

"Yeah, well, you can't believe everything you see at the movies, huh?" Dax made a small toasting gesture, then gulped his bourbon.

"Right," Sanders chuckled. "Um, say, I've always wanted to ask you, when you negotiated the release of the colonist hostages on Titan, how did you—"

Dax couldn't take any more. "Whoa, whoa, kid. Calm down." He turned around, getting a good look at his young fan for the first time. "How old are you?"

"Eighteen, sir."

"Wow. Okay, and you want to be all you can be, huh?"

"Absolutely. I'd like to follow in your footsteps. I mean, I'm trying. I even talked to Captain Sykes about joining your medical support team at—"

Dax cut him off with a dismissive laugh. "You want to follow in my footsteps?" *That's just great,* Dax thought. This was the Alliance's dream come true. Fresh faces eager to join the cause. A dream that Dax had helped build, not that he bothered to ever let the gravity of that notion sink in, save for a few of the longer, darker nights at the bottom of a bottle.

"Here's what you do, Sanders. Keep your head down. Don't get it shot off. War's over, so you shouldn't have too much trouble. Just jump when they tell you to jump, salute when they tell you to salute . . . Oh, and don't buy those tooth-brushes they're selling with my face on 'em. I hear they're get-ting recalled. Some kind of chemical on them or something." He finished his drink and made a break for the exit, patting Sanders on the shoulder as he passed him.

The corporal stood lost in thought, processing the unex-pected words from his hero. "Sir!" Dax turned with a sigh. "I think I understand," Sanders continued, his enthusiasm restored. "The best way to be a hero is to be a good officer, follow orders, and maintain discipline."

Dax shrugged. "Yeah, sure. That's what I was going for."

CHAPTER 6

AN IMPATIENT POUNDING came from outside. A cellblock guard approached and slid open the peephole. Ertac the Darshyll giant stood in the rain on the other side. The guard jerked back as Ertac's wet snout closed in on the peephole.

"Transfer."

The guard unlocked the armored door as another guard stood nearby, rifle at the ready. Ertac moved in, pushing a shackled Eyldwan ahead of him. The cellblocks in the Pit were massive multistory cylinders, carved out of the mountains and reinforced. This made for a deafening echo chamber when the inmates were in an uproar, as they were now while Eyldwan walked the line. As the group of four moved through the processing area, he discretely slipped his hands out of the unlocked shackles.

Ertac made the first move, locking the guard in front of him in a sleeper hold. Immediately, Eyldwan roped the second guard's neck with the chains from his shackles. Both were dispatched in mere moments, but not before one managed to strain out a curse to Ertac: *"Lut-chak't!"* Traitor.

Ertac took a key card from his victim's belt and tossed it to Eyldwan. Grabbing the fallen guard's rifle, he headed into the nearby monitoring station, a control and surveillance post for the guards. A bank of monitors glowed off to the side. He moved quickly to the weapons lockers on the wall, punching in a security code on the keypad and revealing a row of pulse rifles ready for the taking.

Eyldwan continued down the corridor of cells, unlocking the gates one by one with the key card. The noise was maddening. Cheers, shouts, and angry or desperate calls from other convicts demanding their freedom. The former general chose carefully, recalling every face he had studied in preparation for this day. He would need every able body he could spare, but many were simple madmen, liable to deviate to their own petty impulses at a moment's notice.

Ertac remained at the guard post, monitoring as reinforcements began to close in from the adjacent cellblocks. "We must leave, General!"

Outside, the rainstorm raged the landscape. Only the facility's blaring alarms could be heard over the cacophony as the main gate began to lower. Eyldwan waited calmly behind it as Ertac and several freed inmates stood with pulse rifles raised, ready for anything.

The first shot caught one of the inmates in the head, taking him down instantly. The rest turned and exchanged fire with a trio of guards, firing and maintaining cover by the facility's entrance. Out of the rain above, a small transport shuttle flew into view and maneuvered into a hover in front of Eyldwan's group. The inmates continued spraying cover fire as they began to board the craft. As Eyldwan climbed in, he exchanged an acknowledging nod with the pilot, Khern.

The group would suffer two more casualties before the remaining survivors boarded and the shuttle blasted off into the storm, leaving the guards staring at the night sky. The group cheered and yelled obscenities, let out primal shouts of victory, and so on. Eyldwan remained silent in the copilot seat, staring ahead with razor focus, his next target in his mind's eye.

Cartaan. The Carteagan homeworld. News of the prison break traveled through swift but quiet channels to the Cartaan capitol building. President Aarkhan, still adjusting to his new station, requested the incident be kept from the Alliance until an internal investigation could provide at least some answers. In short, the less he appeared caught with his pants down, the better.

"I want a full investigation at the mine," Aarkhan ordered. "Find out how many escaped and who helped them." A young advisor followed at his heels, continuing to take notes as Aarkhan settled into his office desk.

"Yes, sir." As the advisor exited the office, the butt end of a rifle slammed across his face, knocking him cold. His attacker stood in the doorway, remaining in the shadows.

Aarkhan leapt to his feet. "Guards!"

"I wouldn't bother," the voice said calmly. "My men have already taken the building. I could stage a coup right now, but that is not what I wish." He stepped closer, into the light. Aarkhan couldn't hide his shock.

"Utynai."

"Please, sit."

The Carteagan president stared back, fighting the intimidation, until Eyldwan repeated himself menacingly. "Sit."

He obeyed.

"*President* Aarkhan," Eyldwan mockingly addressed him. "There's a reason why they forced that label on you. Have you truly no loyalty to the empire?"

"There is no empire anymore."

"No, there is not."

Aarkhan tensed as the disgraced general slowly approached. It was as if he were seeing a ghost. Worse, a demon resurrected, and only hardened further from the depths of hell.

"What is this? Why have you come here?"

"I come with opportunity. An opportunity to aid a new empire, and all I ask for is a ship."

"And why would I do that?"

"Do you enjoy being their domesticated beast?" Eyldwan chastised. "Waiting for your owner to grant you pats on the head? They are not the kind benefactors they claim." He leaned over the desk, eyes locked with Aarkhan's. "Grant me a warship, and I will restore this world to its rightful place."

"You're mad." Aarkhan nearly stuttered in terror.

"You know I can simply take it, just as I took this building. This wretched symbol of your so-called Alliance. But I had hoped you would see reason."

"Reason?" The president finally found his strength, firing his words back at Eyldwan. "You want to bring war back to Cartaan? Whatever you're planning, whatever followers you have in this madness, you will accomplish nothing."

"More will join us. When I show them the stars again. The glory of the true Cartaan will be remembered by a few, then many. And *we* will lead the galaxy to *our* greatness. Not Earth-kind. Not the Alliance."

He turned his gaze at the far wall of the presidential office. Two banners hung above the entrance, one belonging to the Alliance and, below it, the flag of the old Carteagan Empire. "With your aid or not, the empire will be reborn." With Eyldwan's attention turned, Aarkhan used the opportunity to cautiously scramble for a dagger sheathed underneath his desk.

"I will ask one last time. Will you aid us and be a true son of Cartaan again?"

Aarkhan gripped the dagger hard. "I cannot."

He made his move, slashing wildly. Eyldwan expertly swatted it away, pulled his own blade from his belt and buried it in Aarkhan's chest.

"As the new Cartaan rises, there will be no room for the weak, for detractors." The president collapsed back in his seat, seizing in shock and agony. Eyldwan pushed the blade in farther. "This is necessary. This is necessary, and I am not sorry."

Thirty minutes after Aarkhan's term of office was cut short, capitol security would report several guards found dead at a military shipyard, and one vessel missing. A big one.

CHAPTER 7

THE CEASE-FIRE ANNIVERSARY arrived with plenty of fanfare, as promised. Promotional ads played day and night on every channel, inviting one and all to the festivities. Events were scheduled for a solid month, spread out across the Territories. Dax groaned at the long tour of appearances ahead of him, but he kept his eye on the prize with a postcard from Saleon in his jacket pocket, featuring the beachfront property that awaited him.

"Through struggle, strength. Through honor, remembrance. Through courage, triumph. The United Territories Alliance invites you to—"

"Join in the celebration of ten years of peace. Blah, blah, blah." Dax mockingly talked over the announcements. *Those ads are going to drive me nuts,* he thought. Whether he liked it or not, he knew the words by heart, like a song repeating on the radio until the radio gets thrown out the window. He shut the viewscreen off and continued his approach down to the planet Vega VI. The Vega Memorial Grounds were a long-decaying reminder of the war, until a few short years ago when the rubble was cleared out and the surrounding area revitalized as a sizable public park and event space, complete with an open-air stadium. The celebrations would kick off here with a battle reenactment, a tribute to the veterans, and, of course, a lengthy speech or two by the Hero of the Alliance himself. Dax followed the rest of the incoming transports, landing the *Crichton* in the shipyards behind the venue.

The stands filled up with both public and military onlookers as the morning stretched to noon. At ground level, a platoon of cadets scrambled around making final preparations for the reenactment. "Fall in!" someone announced as Dax approached. The young men and women stood at attention.

"All right, people," he started, warming up his command voice. "Today you will be reenacting the ground battle that was fought ten years ago on the very ruins this memorial was built on. Some of your mothers and fathers may have even been there, and today we will honor them together." Whispers near the back of the group caused a small but noticeable break of laughter.

Dax sighed quietly to himself as he made eye contact with the three troublemakers in the back row. Two immediately straightened up. One stared smugly right back at him. Dax slowly moved to him straight through the rest of the cadets, forcing them to part around him. He had seen Bennett do the same intimidating move several times over, to uppity servicemen and civilians alike. It was a good move. The cadet, however, did not flinch.

"Something funny, cadet?"

"No, sir. Not at all, Commander," he sarcastically replied.

"You know, some brave soldiers gave their lives on this scrap of land. I hope you can show them some respect today."

"Oh, you mean brave soldiers like you? Oh, wait, right, you were busy battling mercs on Titan, or saving the crew of the *Alexandra*." The others tensed up as he carried on. It wasn't so funny anymore. "No, that was early in the war. By then you were posing for a cereal box, maybe?"

Dax stepped closer to the cadet, spotting the name on his uniform. "You got a problem with me, Vasquez?"

"I just find it funny how everywhere I go I hear about the great Commander Harrison, but I don't think I've met anyone who remembers you out on a battlefield . . . sir."

Were he not being such a prick about it, Dax would have admired the cadet's gutsy insubordination. "If you want stories from the war, I can recommend a good book to pass time in the brig. In the meantime, do your duty, Cadet."

Dax started back toward the facility interior, hearing the scattered "oohs" from Vasquez's squad mates under their breath, teasing him like a student called to the principal's office. Still, Vasquez defiantly called out.

"You and Command may have the civvies fooled, but not us, Commander."

Dax ignored him and kept walking. *Great start to the day.*

Minutes later, after briefly getting lost in the halls, he entered the facility operations room. Technicians busied themselves at monitoring stations, communicating with the ground team outside. Overseeing them was Logan, who spotted Dax as soon as he walked in.

"Commander Harrison. First Lieutenant Logan Weaver. I've been assigned to you for the duration of the campaign."

"Oh, a pleasure, Lieutenant. Call me Dax."

A glint of his trademark charm shone from his grin, but Logan continued on, unaffected. "We'll be providing support for the ground reenactment from here and clearing shuttles for aerial maneuvers later."

Without warning, save for a muffled grumbling heard from the hallway, O'Reilly barged into the operations room, Sanders following close behind.

"I don't give a damn whose ass you kissed. I don't need an assistant. And if I did—no offense, Sanders, but you wouldn't be my first choice."

Logan did her best to salvage first impressions. "Commander, this is our medical chief from Central, Doctor Dan O'Reilly. Doctor, this—"

"Yeah, yeah, I know who you are, Harrison. Forgive me if I don't swoon." The old physician clearly had zero interest in putting on airs. Dax smiled genuinely. It was refreshing. "Look, if someone breaks something, I'll be in the infirmary. Until then, I'll be in the infirmary, napping."

O'Reilly left as quickly as he entered, elaborating his complaints in the hallway to no one in particular. "Celebrating peace by playing war . . . ridiculous waste of time . . ."

"Cozy bunch," Dax chuckled.

"Sorry, Commander."

It took a second, but Dax almost managed to remember the young corporal's name. "Sandler?"

"Sanders," he corrected. "And don't worry about a thing, Commander. I'll stick around here, and if you need anything, don't hesitate to ask. Really, anything at all—"

"That's great, Sanders!" Dax cut him off before all of space and time ended around them. "That's great. Why don't you just hang back here and, um . . . monitor the comms team, and I'll let you know when I need you."

"Yes, sir. Absolutely, sir." Sanders hovered behind the technicians as a few of them appeared annoyed by their new unofficial supervisor.

Dax joined Logan at the front of the room, overlooking the stadium through a wall-sized window.

"Not sure who's worse anymore," he whispered. "The fans or the critics."

"I wouldn't know, sir," Logan replied, smiling politely. An awkward moment passed, as the two appeared clueless where to proceed with further small talk. "I must admit, though, I have actually heard some impressive stories myself."

"Oh yeah?" Dax responded, but he was already disinterested with the conversation, as his eyes wandered to a female comms technician nearby.

"My father was on the *Alexandra*."

Suddenly, she had his full attention. He spun around to face her. "Really? And, um, what did he tell you?"

"He said you saved the day."

"Well, there were a lot of brave souls on that ship. I simply did my part," he said, delivering the line with calculated humbleness. "I'm afraid I wasn't personally acquainted with your father, but I'm sure he made you proud."

"He did, sir." She left it at that, but Dax kept a wary eye on her, sensing his every move being analyzed. Or maybe he was just being paranoid. Regardless, he reminded himself that he need only smile for the cameras for a short while longer, and then he could sneak away to a private beach somewhere. No cameras. No Alliance. Just the sand and waves, and hopefully good domestic beer, or a decent selection of imports.

As the opening ceremonies commenced down on Vega, the engineers on Comms Relay Station V-3827 felt a deep rumbling. Seconds later, their final moments would be spent witnessing a giant shadow overtaking the viewports, followed by a large energy weapon powering up and firing in their direction.

The technician who previously caught Dax's eye tapped away at her monitoring tools as system alerts popped up on the screen in front of her.

"Lieutenant, we just lost our long-range comms."

Logan stepped over. "Try a different frequency?"

"I'm doing that, ma'am. So far, it looks like everything is down."

Light-years away, at Central Station, the large aerial screens above the promenade all displayed a digital video scramble and an error message: "SATELLITE LINK LOST." Sykes stared grimly at his own scrambled screen on the wall of his office.

"Oh, Dax. Don't tell me you broke something already."

The cadets on the ground of the stadium felt it first, followed shortly by the spectators in the stands and the control room personnel. A rumbling shook the entire memorial grounds, and slowly everyone looked to the sky. The clouds above buckled, and through them descended a massive warship, the entire stadium falling under its shadow.

Dax stood in awe along with the rest of the control room, mouth agape. "That's big. Is that part of the show?" Logan's expression answered no, and she wasted no time in her response. She turned back to the communications tech.

"Any luck with those comms?"

"No, ma'am. Still short-wave only."

"Patch me in. Emergency frequency." The tech did so, and Logan tapped the comms pin on her uniform. "Attention, any Alliance fleet in the area. This is Lieutenant Logan Weaver. We have a large, unidentified Carteagan vessel violating airspace at Vega Memorial. Battle class. Requesting assist—"

She paused as a large whirring sound filled the air outside. The ship's main cannon glowed with energy for a few brief seconds and blasted a crater in the middle of the field below. Anyone who wasn't already running for their lives was most certainly doing so now.

Screams of horror filled the stadium. The warship continued its assault, firing wildly at the troops on the ground as well as the fleeing spectators. As the cannon slowly circled the facility, a blast struck near the ops room. Logan dove for cover as the giant window shattered, raining deadly shards around her. She shouted again into her comm.

"We are under attack! Repeat, we are under attack!" She glanced around. The comms team members helped each other to their feet. Sanders peeked out from a console where he had taken cover. And, and—*Where the hell is Harrison?*

Dax bolted through the hallway, running like hell for the exit. He darted frantically through the facility corridors, passing O'Reilly, who had stumbled out of the infirmary.

"What the hell is going on out there?!"

"Uh . . . gotta go!" Dax continued at full speed.

Logan stood by the door of the control room, ushering everyone out. "Go! Get to evac shuttles! Take as many as you can with you!" On the short-wave monitors, a voice began to break through the ongoing static.

"This is . . . Alliance patrol. . . . Do you copy . . . ? Repeat . . ."

Logan scrambled to the console.

"This is Lieutenant Weaver. I copy, patrol."

" . . . received your transmission . . . En route to memorial . . . ETA ten minutes . . . Get your people out of there, Weaver."

Dax dashed through the shipyards. The continued assault rumbled the ground beneath him. He flinched and ducked for cover among the transports as the nearby explosions filled his ears.

"SAMM, open up!" He continued his mad dash to the *Crichton* as the cargo ramp began to lower.

O'Reilly stormed into the operations room. "Sanders!"

"Sir, what are you still doing here?"

"Getting you, you idiot. Come on!" He grabbed Sanders by the arm, but the corporal turned around for a final check of the room. The last of the techs had made their way out. Logan, however, remained at a comms console.

"Lieutenant, I think we better leave now!"

"I'm sending the shuttles emergency routes. They can regroup at—"

"They're already on the move!" O'Reilly shouted. "And we need to be too if we're going to make it in time. Let's go, Weaver!"

Finally, she relented. She moved to a weapons locker against the wall. An eye scanner confirmed her authorization, and seconds later she headed toward the exit with a rifle at the ready. "Follow me."

Several emergency transports took to the sky, leaving the *Crichton* on the ground. The engines whirred and sputtered out. Dax tried again, flipping the ignition controls back and forth and hoping for a miracle. No response.

"Why aren't we in the air, SAMM?"

"We have a burnout in the port engine. Redirecting power—"

"Just make it happen!"

With most of the stadium emptied, hardly anyone remained to witness Eyldwan and several of his crew enter the facility. They emerged with a large storage container in tow. Alliance markings peeked out from underneath a tarp covering the object. From the warship above, a cargo lift descended to the stadium, meeting the mercenaries as they walked onto the field. In moments, they loaded the container and rode the lift back up toward the ship with not a soul to contest them.

"All too easy," Eyldwan gloated.

Logan entered the shipyard first, rifle up, scanning for hostiles. All clear. The trio rushed out, just in time to see the last of the transports taking off. Sanders desperately tried to flag down the pilot.

"Wait!" he shouted, waving his arms.

O'Reilly did the same, less politely. "Wait, goddammit!"

Logan caught the vessel's ID number on its hull and tapped her comms pin. "Transport ET175, lower your cargo lift. We have Alliance personnel on the ground!"

"Copy—"

BOOM! The pilot's last word rang in Logan's ears as a laser blast blanketed the transport in fire. ET175 spun out of control before going down hard, mere yards ahead of the group. They ran for cover, turning to the source of the blast. The warship, cargo now loaded, had repositioned to make its exit and was now directly facing them.

With nowhere to run, Logan, Sanders, and O'Reilly watched the great ship approach, expecting the next blast to hit at any second. Just as all seemed lost, three Alliance fighters soared in from behind them. The patrol. They opened fire on the warship, sweeping by at full throttle.

"Yeah!" Sanders raised a triumphant fist to the sky, cheering in his ever-optimistic fashion. O'Reilly remained grim, with a more realistic view of the evolving situation. The three small one-man fighters would serve as a momentary distraction at best. He looked to Logan for options.

"Well, now what?"

Now what, indeed. They had no options. And it was then that Logan heard the faint whirring engine of the *Crichton*, sputtering to life at the far end of the shipyard.

"That's what I wanted to hear!" Dax was elated to finally hear the sweet sound of the engines firing. "Let's go!" He gripped the yoke, ready to take off, when a voice came through the comms.

"Commander! Commander Harrison, are you in there?"

Dax pulled up a video monitor of the ship exterior. Logan desperately pounded at the cargo ramp door. Up ahead, the warship was closing in fast. Dax sensed the moment of truth. He hated moments of truth. *Oh shit.*

The cargo ramp lowered. Logan, O'Reilly, and Sanders rushed inside.

The fight raged on in the skies above. As expected, the patrol ships continued their strafing runs but did little damage to the Carteagan behemoth. One of them took a deadly hit and crashed down into the stadium grounds.

Dax tensed up as his new passengers made their way to the bridge. He readied his command voice.

Logan entered at the head of the pack. "Harrison!"

"Well, there you are!" Dax shouted back. "It's about time!"

"Where the hell—"

"Just shut up and hold on to something!" He cut her off before she could finish the question, buying more time to work out an explanation.

He hit the throttle hard. Logan and O'Reilly braced themselves on their surroundings. Sanders stumbled back into SAMM and grabbed on for dear life. SAMM's holographic displays lit up.

"Greetings. I would advise strapping into a vacant seat to avoid injuries during takeoff." The voice startled him, loosening his grip and sending him flying back, appropriately enough, into a vacant seat at the back of the cockpit.

The *Crichton* soared up out of the atmosphere, trailing behind the other fleeing transports. A blast suddenly caught their backside, and Dax's monitors confirmed the warship was still in pursuit, attempting to pick off the escaping fleet.

Everyone braced from the jolt of the blast. The cockpit lights flickered, and a rapid alert blared from the console.

Sanders panicked. "Are we hit?!"

"No! The ship's just blowing up for fun!" Dax shook his head at the inane question. Another blast sent them reeling. He strapped into his seat and the others followed suit.

"Does this piece of junk go any faster?"

"Doc, you make me laugh, but don't push it!"

Logan cut through the bickering. "Does your ship have a jump drive?"

"It's charging. All we have to do is not die for another . . . thirty seconds." Those seconds seemed to last a lifetime. Dax turned his rage to the alarm still blaring at him, pounding his fist on the console.

"SAMM, if you don't shut this thing up, I'm gonna break it!" It stopped immediately.

"Alarms silenced," SAMM announced. "Ten seconds to jump, Commander." Everyone braced as he made the final countdown. "Hyperspace jump in three, two, o—"

Another blast interrupted the count. Sparks flew and the cockpit lights blacked out entirely. Sanders let out a high-pitched scream, and the *Crichton* vanished from space in a momentary blur of light.

CHAPTER 8

NIDAHNA PASSED NERVOUSLY through the wards, observing the buzz of activity around her. Residents of Central Station gathered around screens in the halls and throughout the promenade, debating what foolish technical glitch may have caused the universal interruption of the broadcast. At last, she reached her personal quarters and moved swiftly inside.

"Lock." The door system responded with a chime. Nidahna stood alone in the dimly lit room, wringing her hands and taking a minute to focus herself. She moved to her personal tablet on the nightstand, and a few commands later, she was face-to-face with a holographic transmission of Eyldwan.

"I expected your call," he snarled.

Nidahna maintained her composure, despite his intimidating presence. "It is done then?"

"We have accomplished our first task, but our mission is far from over."

"Then you have what you needed. Release them."

"We may require your services yet. They will be released at my discretion and no sooner."

Nidahna shut her eyes and clenched her jaw, fighting back any hint of tears. She fully expected the answer, but it still wounded her. "You will receive no aid from Cartaan. Our people will not betray the peace treaty. President Aarkhan—"

"Cartaan will be seeking new leadership shortly. President Aarkhan was . . . disagreeable. Unfortunate actions were necessary." Eyldwan gazed at her suspiciously. "Your precious Alliance has already betrayed the treaty, has it not? Why do you rush to their defense?"

If there was ever a moment to make a case for reason, this was it. Nidahna chose her words carefully. "The humans struggle, but they wish for peace. We are the same. No better, no worse."

He glared at her with fire in his eyes. "Never compare me to a human again."

Nidahna knew any further discussion would be pointless, and she dared not continue provoking him. The strength in her voice began to falter, as her thoughts turned to more important matters. "May I see them?"

Eyldwan signaled a tech to make the arrangements, and the feed switched to a young Carteagan girl, no older than nine. "Mother?"

Nidahna smiled. "Bila! Are you all right, my love?"

"Yes, but there are these men here. They said they know you, but I've never seen them before. They won't leave and they won't say why they're here."

"They . . . they're just there to look after you while I'm away."

"But Fira'ni always watches us."

"She's not feeling well. Listen to me, Bila. I need you to look after Ranni. Keep him close. He needs you."

Bila looked to her younger brother, Ranni, across the room, barely a toddler. He played with his toys, oblivious to Eyldwan's pair of mercenaries keeping watch. Nidahna was trying her hardest not to alarm her, but it was clear Bila sensed the danger. "What's going on? I'm scared."

"Nothing. Everything is fine, my love. Don't worry. I'll be home soon." The feed cut back to Eyldwan, and Nidahna glared at him with a mother's ferocity. "What have you done with my children's caretaker?"

"She was . . . also disagreeable. I would advise you to keep your children in mind should you have any notions of disobeying me. I do not wish it, but my men have no problem taking further . . . unfortunate actions."

The *Crichton* exploded out of hyperspace in an uncontrolled spin. The crew reeled in the spiraling cockpit as Dax attempted to regain control.

"Systems restoring," SAMM announced. "Running diagnostics." Dax leveled the ship, much to everyone's relief, but they sensed a new problem.

Sanders squirmed in his seat. "Why do I feel funny?" He then watched dumbfounded as Dax's empty liquor bottle floated past him then smashed to the ground.

"SAMM?" Dax knew he wasn't going to like the news.

"Hull is intact, but artificial gravity has been compromised."

"Oh, great."

SAMM's repair subroutines hit a wall. "I'm afraid my connections are severed, Commander. You will need to make the repairs locally."

Logan righted herself in her seat. "Gravity drive's out?"

"Not out. Fluxing. Keep your straps on." Dax unstrapped himself and headed to the back of the cockpit.

"I can help," Sanders blurted.

"Fine, hold this." Dax grabbed a tool bag from an overhead compartment and tossed it at him, and the two made their way into the ship's interior. SAMM's voice followed them through the hall via the *Crichton*'s comms systems.

"A word of caution: gravity fluctuations will increase in strength in proximity to the damage."

Sanders secured the tool bag over his shoulder. "That means it's going to get worse?"

"Hope you got a strong stomach," Dax chuckled.

A sudden intense gravity increase yanked the two men to the deck, and the side of Dax's face slammed on the floor. "Ahh! . . . And a strong head." They pressed on, crawling with the new weight on their backs.

Back in the cockpit, Logan unstrapped herself and moved to the main console. O'Reilly looked on with a disapproving eye.

"What are you doing?"

"Figuring out where we are and what the hell is going on."

"Those croc-bug bastards just declared war! That's what's going on."

Logan paid no mind and tapped away at the screens. The computer went to work triangulating their new location, and a chirping sound signaled its success.

"We jumped to the Argos sector. That just might be close enough to reach Central." She continued at the console, looking for long-range comms controls.

Still stuck to the floor, Dax strained to reach the door panel to the engine room. His outstretched fingers just managed to touch the panel when the gravity completely reversed, sending him, Sanders, and the tool bag to the ceiling with a painful thud.

"Are you serious?!" If they hadn't just been attacked, Dax would've assumed SAMM was simply toying with him now.

Logan sat, exasperated and having no luck at communications. "Any Alliance personnel in the vicinity, come in. This is Lieutenant Weaver on the cargo vessel *Crichton*." She continued to be met with nothing but static.

O'Reilly remained seated. "Forget it, Weaver. They must've taken out the relays before the attack. We're not reaching anybody out here."

A moment later, a voice broke through the static. "I copy, Weaver."

The voice was masked by static, but it sounded small. Like a child's voice. Logan exchanged confused looks with O'Reilly before she responded. "Who is this?"

"Communications Officer Kiko, Lieutenant."

"Are you stationed nearby, Officer?"

"Yes, sir. I mean, ma'am. Comms Relay 742 operating for Argos sector. Do you need assistance?"

Logan thought a moment before replying. Whoever it was on the other end, it was a friendly voice in the middle of nowhere. "Um, yes. We are in an emergency situation. Requesting permission to dock for repairs."

"Transmitting coordinates now. See you soon, *Crichton*."

The engine room door opened, and Dax and Sanders walked in along the ceiling. Dax looked around. It had been a good long while since he'd had to make any manual repairs. "All right, SAMM, what are we looking for here?"

"A large panel located above the starboard engine."

"Okay, starboard. This way." Dax began moving to his right. Sanders stopped him, pointing to their left.

"Sir, isn't it this way?"

"Starboard is right. Right?" Dax second-guessed himself as he said it.

"Normally, yes, but we're facing the rear of the ship."

"Yeah, but we're upside-down and facing—SAMM, which one is it?"

"Continue to your right, Commander." Dax pointed a triumphant finger in Sanders's face with a matching "Ha." They located the wall panel, and Dax went to work prying the stubborn cover open. As soon as it popped loose, a wave of sparks flew past his face from the damaged wires inside. He jumped back, involuntarily letting out a short but high-pitched shout. Sanders remained quiet, but Dax felt the silent judgment. He cleared his throat as low and manly as he could before continuing.

"Connect red to blue to engage environmental backup systems," SAMM instructed. "This will stabilize artificial gravity until further repairs are completed."

"Right, got it. Here we go. Sanders, tools."

Sanders handed him a wire cutter from the tool kit. Dax snipped the red wire, causing the gravity to zero. Both men began slowly drifting off the ceiling. Dax held on to the panel, reorienting himself right side up. Sanders found himself with nothing to hold on to and drifted helplessly, awkwardly flapping his arms.

"Uh, Commander?"

"Just relax, Sanders. Try to swim yourself straight."

"I, uh, I can't swim, sir." Dax looked at him strangely. *How'd this kid make it through the academy?* He finished the repairs, twisting the two wires firmly together. Gravity restored through the entire ship, landing Dax safely on his feet and Sanders flat on his back.

"Ha! Piece of cake! Sanders?"

The corporal replied from the floor with a groan.

Minutes later, they emerged from the engine room, meeting Logan and O'Reilly in the interior walkway.

"Finally," O'Reilly grumbled.

"We're all clear," Dax proudly announced. "Or back to limping anyway. What's going on? Where are we?"

"Argos. En route to a local comms station. We can report to Central and assess the damage from there." It seemed Logan had done the heavy lifting for him. He could get used to this.

"Good. Perfect. Um, good work, Weaver."

"Assess the damage?" O'Reilly fumed. "How about destroying a ten-year cease-fire and everything we've built? Those *dey-nok-shota*!"

Dax looked at him with amusement. "Doc, was that a Carteagan swear?"

"The name of the language is Cardic, Harrison. And yes, they do have some good ones. I'll give them that." He noticed Sanders rubbing the back of his ailing head. "What's with you?"

"I'm fine, just a little banged up."

The doctor knew a stubborn patient when he saw one. "I think I spotted a med bay back there."

"Down and to the right," Dax directed.

"Come on, boy. Let's see what you broke."

Now that their path was set, Logan's doubts flooded back to the front of her mind. She had some serious pointed questions to ask. She waited until she believed the others were out of earshot. "Commander, I think we need to discuss—"

"The Carteagans, right. Unbelievable, and after years of peace—"

"We don't know who was responsible, which is why we need to reach Central. But, sir, that's not what I wanted to discuss."

"Well, spit it out then, Weaver."

"Well, sir, with all due respect, I was wondering what happened to you during the attack."

"What do you mean?"

"I mean, we were attacked, I turned, and you were gone."

Dax could see she meant business. Indignation was his only defense. "I was making sure those civilians were getting to their transports, and with the last one leaving, I was trying to get airborne myself! You're lucky I stuck around so long. I thought you'd have evacuated by then too." Logan eyed him suspiciously, and he doubled down by pulling rank. "Are you accusing me of something, Lieutenant?"

"No, sir. Just trying to make sense of it all."

"Look, we're all shook up. Let's get to the station and figure out our next move."

"Yes, sir." She kept a cautious eye on him as he headed back to the cockpit. Once he was alone, Dax took a long deep breath. His bad day was getting worse by the minute.

A proximity alarm beeped on the wall display until a weather-beaten hand shut it off. Dern looked ahead at the *Crichton*, which had just completed its landing in the docking bay. His docking bay. "What the hell is this?"

The scraggly middle-aged man gave a look about as charming as his personality: not very. He met the crew head-on as they emerged from the beat-up old freighter.

"Hi there! Lieutenant Commander Dax Harrison—"

"Whoa, whoa, whoa. I don't give a damn who you are. What do you think you're doing making an unauthorized landing on my station?"

Logan stepped closer. "We were directed here for repairs. Spoke to an Officer Kiko."

"Officer?" Dern's eyes widened in disbelief. "Kiko! Front and center!"

A timid eleven-year-old girl peeked out from the cargo bay entrance.

"Now," he added with a parental tone. Kiko walked over, hanging her head in guilt. Dax grinned at Logan.

"*This* is the officer you spoke to?"

"She offered assistance. In case you noticed, we need some. Sir."

Dern grabbed Kiko forcefully. "What did I say about staying off the comms?" He scolded. "Huh? How many times? What kind of trouble are you trying to bring here?"

"Hey, hey, calm down!" Dax directed the attention off the poor young girl. "Look, I didn't catch your name, Mr. . . . ?"

"Dern. Chief engineer."

"Okay, listen, Dern. Trouble is headed your way whether you like it or not. See my ship? That's from a little run-in we just had with some pretty pissed-off Carteagans who, as far as we can tell, just decided to throw the cease-fire out the window!"

"They attacked civilians on Vega VI," Logan added. "We barely made it out ourselves."

"Well, it's a good thing I didn't enlist," Dern snapped. "Because this is a civilian outpost, and I don't take orders from you. Go do your job, and let me do mine."

"Hey!" O'Reilly marched straight up to the engineer's face. "You want to bury your head in the sand, fine. But guess what? These croc-hoppers chasing us? They wiped out all the local comms to cover their tracks. Which means eventually they'll be coming this way too. Probably on the way as we speak."

Dax watched as Dern processed the situation. It was a serious moment, but for a second he wished he had some popcorn. It was a battle of the curmudgeons.

"Now do you want to keep wasting time," O'Reilly continued, "or would you rather help us patch up our ship? And then maybe, maybe we might just find some room to take you with us."

Dern looked around. All eyes were on him, and he was outnumbered.

"Well then," he begrudgingly resigned. "What can we do for *the* Commander Harrison and his crew?"

CHAPTER 9

YOUNG "OFFICER" KIKO received a smaller additional scolding from Dern a short while later, but they moved on after that. Still, she could sense his tension as they examined the damage along the *Crichton*'s hull.

"Whoa!" She gazed at the extensive laser burns, unable to contain her excitement. "Is that pulse blasts? Looks like pulse blasts. They got hit hard on this side. That's crazy! I bet that engine's dead, but we got the parts, I think. I can't believe we're gonna fix the *Crichton*!"

"Kiko," Dern stopped her in his usual tone. "If you're babbling, you're not focusing." It was his mantra. Kiko had heard it a million times over, and it deflated her enthusiasm for the time being. Still, she was used to it, and she knew it was best to simply give him his quiet time to think.

Instead, she worked up the courage to talk to Dax and asked if he'd like to help her find the parts she needed. Minutes later, she led him down the dark stairwell into her workshop.

"Thanks."

"For what?"

"Stopping my uncle."

"That guy's your uncle? Not very nice, is he?"

Kiko shrugged. "I dunno. He just gets mad sometimes."

"Just you two here? That's gotta drive you nuts."

"Not a lot to it. The comms practically run themselves. But I keep busy." The automatic lights flickered on as they entered, revealing a treasure trove of tinkering. Gadgets, projects, and miscellaneous junk littered their surroundings.

"Holy crap. You're not kidding." Kiko smiled with pride as Dax took it all in. "Jeez, kid. Is this your personal junkyard?"

Her smile faded. "What? I like making stuff. Not like there's anything else to do around here." Dax followed her through the maze of junk, nearly tripping on scattered parts in his path. He took note of a series of numbered tags on some of the more interesting items. #1, #2, #3, and so on.

"And what's all this?"

"Stuff I'm still working on. Engine parts are this way." Arriving at a workbench, she picked up a large roll of paper resting nearby and rolled it out. Dax leaned in to see a giant inventory list. Very thorough, very organized, and decorated with doodles of flowers and spaceships along the edges.

"You sure we're going to find anything useful in this heap?"

"Sure! Just gotta find 'em." The edges of the sheet rolled back. Kiko mashed the paper down with her palm, but it refused to lie flat. Instead, she tried reaching for an item resting on the top shelf of the bench. The metallic lunchbox-shaped object was just out of reach.

"Grab that for me?" Dax did so, trying not to let his strain show with the surprisingly heavy object. He quickly set it on the paper's edge with a thud. As he caught his breath, he noticed a #7 tag attached to it, and the curiously familiar design of the hardware began to sink in.

"Is . . . is that a hyperdrive?"

"Um, yeah. G-series."

"You're using a Galaxy-class hyperdrive as a paperweight."

The young girl looked up from her inventory sheet. "What? It works. And it's pretty."

Dax stared at the nonchalant child, his anxiety kicking up. "Is that thing functional?"

"I dunno, maybe." She shrugged. "I patched it up, but I got nothing to test it on."

"You know how valuable that is? Those things move flagships. You could probably move this whole station if you attached an engine to it."

Kiko's eyes widened with excitement. "Really?"

"Forget I said that! It's dangerous . . . and probably leaking radiation. I'm standing over here." Kiko rolled her eyes as he moved to the far side of the bench.

"It's clean. I checked. Jeez, I didn't think you'd be so whiny."

At the far side of the station, Logan and Sanders stood by a bank of communications hardware as Dern checked and rechecked the same tools he had checked and rechecked prior to their arrival. After a series of flipping breakers, twisting knobs, and even a kick or two, Logan broke the silence.

"Long range is down here too?"

Dern gave one more kick for good measure. "Seems to be. Anything past the outer planets went dead six hours ago. I'm guessing that's about when your surprise guests showed up."

"Yeah. There's no way to get anything back to the Sol System?"

"Well, I did have one idea. Kind of a temporary fix, but it requires a ship. Lucky for me—"

Logan smirked. "We brought you a ship."

"Bingo." Dern rubbed his eyes, weary from staring at monitors. "If I can patch into your nav beacon, I'm thinking I can reroute it and push a broadcast through the station comms."

Sanders looked puzzled. "Navigation? Doesn't that just go 'ding'?"

"Well, if we boost the gain enough, you should be able to send more than just a ding. Might still hear the nav, but we can filter it down some. If your friends at Central have half a brain at the controls, they should be able to sync up and reply back."

"Let's do it." This was the best news Logan had heard yet.

"Wait, that's not all. This is the only solution we got, but it's messy," Dern warned. "We start blasting communications on an overloaded nav signal, that's gonna scream interference in all directions. Now if the Carteagans are still in the neighborhood, best case, they hear every word of your little secret powwow. Worst—"

"They track it back to here." Sanders's eyes threatened to bug out of his head.

"We don't have a choice," Logan said, her mind already made up. "The sooner we alert Central, the sooner they can send the fleet out and track the Carteagans down before they attack again."

Dern looked at the overzealous lieutenant, raising an eyebrow and folding his arms across his chest. "Shouldn't we be discussing this with your commander?"

"Leave that to me. Just get it up and running."

He shrugged. "Yes, ma'am." If there would be a battle over the chain of command later, far be it from him to stop the show.

Kiko approached a set of shelves twice as tall as herself, filled with dirty bins of collected engine parts. The method to her madness.

She pointed to the top shelf. "Grab me that one?"

Dax pulled the exceedingly dusty bin down from the shelf, nearly dropping it as he broke into a brief sneezing fit.

"Hold still!" Kiko dug through the pile of hardware. Dax set the heavy bin onto the floor, freeing his hands to bat the flying allergy bombs away from his face.

"Hey, these parts don't look like they're in great shape."

"Well, they're in better shape than your broken ones."

"Fair point," he conceded. "Thanks, by the way, for bringing us in. You didn't have to. You know, your uncle's kind of a jerk, but he's right. We could have been anybody."

Kiko kept digging and setting parts aside, fully engaged in her hunt. "I recognized your ship. I know all about you and the *Crichton* and SAMM. Is he real or just something they made up for the movies?"

"No, SAMM's real. He's on board right now, probably ordering your uncle around with repairs."

Kiko laughed merrily at the image in her head. Dax figured her for a fan when he arrived, noticing an old "Commander Harrison Wants You" recruitment poster in the docking bay when he stepped off the *Crichton*. Something told him it didn't belong to Dern. He watched as the industrious young girl grabbed an old rag from the pocket of her work pants, gave each part a quick wipe down, and tossed the worthy items onto an idling hovercart nearby. The not-so-worthy junk she tossed back into the bin.

"Ooh, T-14 couplings. Catch!" She tossed them to Dax, along with another rag to help with the cleaning.

"Thanks. You're pretty sharp, kid. Your folks didn't put you in the academy?"

"They died in the war."

His hands stopped a moment. "I'm sorry."

"It's all right. I don't really remember them."

It made sense to Dax now. Parents gone, left to her uncle (estranged, he assumed from the attitude) whether he liked it or not. He figured he should say something nice. "Well, I'm sure they would've been proud of the little grease monkey you've become. You know, I'm sort of an orphan myself, actually. I mean, not entirely. Dad left pretty early on, so I don't remember much of him. Mom, well, she did her best, I suppose, but I was mostly on my own by your age. So we got that in common."

Kiko stopped scrubbing. "Not having parents? That's kinda sad."

"Yeah, I guess it kinda is. Sorry, not sure where I was going with that." Dax shook his head, internally scolding himself. He wasn't great at relating. "Well, what I mean to say is, the Alliance took me in when I didn't have anywhere else to go. Now, I'm not saying that's the only way to go, but that was my story, and it might not have happened otherwise. So, you got a bad deal too, but you ended up learning all this useful stuff from your uncle. This could be the start of your amazing story."

Kiko grinned. "So I could end up like you?"

"Maybe, sure."

She started giggling. "With your ship all broken?"

The kid was mocking him, but he took it. "Fair enough. And, hey, case in point. The Alliance could always use more brilliant mechanics—" His comms pin chirped, interrupting him. It was Logan.

"Commander, we're ready to make contact over here."

"On the way." Dax tossed the couplers in the bin and the rag back to Kiko. "Take those to the ship, yeah?"

"Yes, sir," she said with her best obedient cadet voice.

Dax turned back just before he was out the door. "And don't fiddle with anything unless SAMM tells you."

"Aye aye, commander!"

Much to Dern's disappointment, Dax was perfectly fine with Logan's decision to attempt contact with Central. In fact, he seemed content to let her continue making the calls in general with no more than a simple "Sure, that's fine" from him. The less "commander-ing" work he had to do, the better.

The nav reroute solution worked as Dern had promised. He hovered over the controls at the back of the conference room, adjusting and attenuating the signal as Dax, Logan, Sanders, and O'Reilly sat at a round table. Footage from the Vega attack played, projecting above them at the center. The connection stuttered and scrambled every few seconds, but it was enough to get the point across. Bennett and Sykes watched from the other end in Sykes's office.

"Jesus." Bennett grimly watched the footage. "How many did we lose?"

"Can't say for certain," Logan answered. "But at least two fighters and one transport of Alliance and civilians."

Sykes scratched at his jawline stubble in thought. "What the hell are they thinking? Cartaan wouldn't stand a chance against the Alliance systems. Not anymore."

O'Reilly chimed in. "Maybe they think they've got the edge with that monster ship of theirs."

"Any way we can get a closer look at that?"

"This is all we got from the *Crichton*'s surveillance feed," Dax said. "You officially know as much as we do, sir."

"It's tough, but it's not invincible," Logan said. "You'd definitely need more than a few patrol ships to take it out."

Bennett spotted something in the footage. "Go back a second."

Dern rewound until the admiral signaled to stop.

"Right there." The projection froze on an image of Eyldwan and his forces loading the mysterious cargo. Sykes stared at the Carteagan face.

"Can we ID him?"

"No need," Bennett said solemnly. "Eyldwan Utynai."

Dax tried to make sense of the name, completely perplexed. "I'm sorry?"

"He was a *saakesh*," Bennett continued. "Cartaan's equivalent of a general during the war, and probably the most ruthless Carteagan alive."

The admiral transmitted Eyldwan's digital dossier over the projection. Mug shot, name, history, etc. The crew of the *Crichton* gazed at the laundry list of offenses. Even Dern leaned in for a look at the impressively terrifying list. Dax simply continued trying to process the bizarrely alien name.

"Eld . . . Ellydid . . . Oh, screw it. I'll just call him Eyelid."

"His men wiped out entire colonies," Bennett went on. "By the end of it, even his own commanders were sick of him disobeying orders. The Alliance demanded he be held accountable for his war crimes as part of the cease-fire, and the empire handed him over gladly."

Dax scoffed at the war criminal gone loose. "For a man condemned in two worlds, he seems to be doing all right."

Dern looped the footage on the few brief moments of Eyldwan's image. Sanders focused in on the mysterious cargo in tow as Bennett continued.

"Utynai was in the Pit. Lifers colony on SR822. He would've had some serious help to break out of there."

"What's that they're taking?" All eyes fell on Sanders. His eyes widened as the admiral stared back. "S-sorry, sir. I just—" He pointed at the projection. "That right there. It must be important, right? I mean, from the looks of it, they just came out guns blazing for that."

Sykes squinted at the glitching footage. "The Vega memorial is public grounds. There's no military hardware there. Admiral?"

Bennett seemed to take a pause before responding. "I'll have security investigate."

"Admiral, with your permission I'd like to assist—"

"We'll look into it, Lieutenant Weaver. Commander, you and your crew get flying back to base as soon as you're able."

Dax was overjoyed. "Yes, sir!" Finally, he could be done with this mess.

"Mr. Dern, the Alliance thanks you for your assistance."

"Oh, um, no problem, Admiral." Dern awkwardly saluted the projection, unsure if that was the expected protocol.

"Bennett out." The communication ended and the projection faded away. Everyone sat in their thoughts for a moment until Sanders broke the silence.

"What do you think?"

"I think he's full of it," O'Reilly grumbled.

"I'd actually have to agree," Logan said. "I don't know about Captain Sykes, but the admiral knows more than he's saying."

Dax remained completely unfazed. "Well, it's their problem now. How long till we can get out of here?"

"A couple hours at least," Dern said. "Maybe less, if Kiko helps me lock down that port engine."

Dax enthusiastically banged on the table. "All right then! We're home free in a few hours." He shot up out of his seat and headed toward the hall. "It's been fun, everybody. If you'll excuse me, I gotta go see a man about a droid."

Logan followed him out, her eyes locked on and deadly. "Commander!"

Dax turned, still oblivious to her rage. "Yes, Lieutenant?"

"May I ask what you're doing, sir?"

"Well, if it's all that important to you, Weaver, I'm trying to find the damn restroom in this place."

"That's not what I meant. I—" She held her tongue, nearly stuttering with frustration.

Dax looked at her like a crazy person. "What?"

"Permission to speak freely, sir?"

"Granted."

"What the hell is wrong with you?"

"I . . . what . . . you . . ." He had no worthy response. "Permission revoked." He turned and walked away, but the lieutenant followed at his heels.

"Is this a game to you? A war criminal is on the loose and you don't even care?"

"You heard Bennett. They've got it under control. We're going home."

"The fleet is systems away. Who knows what damage will be done by the time they get out here. We're here. We should act now!"

Dax laughed a loud forced laugh as he continued down the hall, half-listening and still searching for the damned restroom. "And what do you expect to do in a half-busted cargo ship? Throw rocks? You wanna take on Eyelid and his army? You go right ahead, but you're going to need another ride because me, SAMM, and the *Crichton* are gone."

Logan's blood boiled. "So that's it. That's the plan from the great Commander Harrison. You're going to run, like you did on Vega?"

"Oh, for the love—"

"No more bullshit! You went running the second that ship showed up. You were leaving us behind!"

Dax continued through a bulkhead door, hoping to escape her. Logan followed him straight into the cargo bay. He threw his hands up incredulously. "I am completely lost in this place."

"*This* is not the Commander Harrison who saved the *Alexandra*, or single-handedly made peace on Titan, or led the rescue ops to extract Darshyll POWs. No, *this* is someone else!"

"Well, gosh, Logan. Why don't you tell me how you really feel? Look, if this is a woman proving her strength thing, you don't have to convince—"

That was it. Logan sucker-punched him square in the jaw. Dax hit the deck hard.

"Son of a bitch! Are you crazy?" Dax reeled from the pain. For starters, it was one hell of a punch. Secondly, it had been a good long time since Dax had been in a scuffle. Since the Hero of the Alliance business started, he more often received drinks rather than punches in bars.

Logan looked down at the mysterious figure on the ground in front of her, her head held high. "My father told me about a man he admired. Someone who inspired others and gave the people hope. *You* are not him." Dax's eyes widened as she pulled her sidearm from the holster against her thigh. "So I want to know who the hell you are, right now."

Kiko, having heard the commotion, emerged from the *Crichton*. She stood in silence, staring on.

"Logan—" Dax began.

"Name, rank, assignment! Are you a spy? Agent of Cartaan?"

The rest entered the docking bay. Dern leaned against the bulkhead, watching casually, amused even. O'Reilly and Sanders moved toward the standoff.

"Weaver!"

"Commander? Lieutenant, what's going on?" Sanders stared at the two like a lost puppy.

Logan kept her pistol trained on the suspected imposter. "This man is not who he says he is. This is not Dax Harrison."

"Yes, I am! Jesus, you need a blood sample to prove it?" Dax patted his busted lower lip and held out a bloody finger. "Here!"

"I suppose I could arrange that." Dax looked at O'Reilly. "A blood test. If you need one, I can make it happen."

Enough was enough. "All right, let's settle this." Dax hoisted himself to his feet and marched to the far wall of the cargo bay. "You see this?" He ripped the old recruitment poster from the wall, the illustrated visage of himself staring back at him. He turned and held it up for everyone to see. "*This* is not Dax Harrison. I am. The *real* Dax Harrison."

He made his way back to Logan, getting up close and personal. "What did you expect? The dashing hero who snaps his fingers and saves the day? Wake up!"

Her eyes burned back at his, but she remained silent. He tossed the poster away. "This isn't real! It's propaganda! The people wanted a hero? Well, they got one, manufactured courtesy of Alliance HQ."

Logan wasn't having it. "You are not Commander Harrison. My father—"

"Your father was paid to keep quiet with the rest of the *Alexandra* crew. I'm sorry, Logan, but your father was a damn liar."

She clenched her fist, readying another swing. A sudden proximity alert startled everyone out of the moment. Dern rushed over to the alarming monitor.

"Ohhhh, no, no, no. Oh shit."

O'Reilly joined him at the console. "Carteagans?"

"Looks like they tracked that signal a lot faster than I thought they would."

The warship approached the station. Eyldwan sat in the captain's chair at the center of his bridge crew. "Open a channel."

Logan rushed to Dern. "Can we get out on the Crichton?"

"That hyperdrive's fried. You think you're gonna outrun them on one engine?"

"Attention, Commander Harrison." Everyone froze as Eyldwan's voice echoed over the station's comms. "The empire thanks you for graciously providing your location. In return, we are prepared to offer you a choice. My men will be boarding the station shortly. Surrender yourself without incident and we shall spare the rest of the lives in your company. Any attempt to resist or escape, and the entire station will be destroyed."

O'Reilly laughed. "Is that all? Fine, take him."

"No!" Kiko dropped her tools and ran to Dax's defense, clinging to his jacket sleeve.

Dax gulped hard. "Um, hang on a sec. What do you want with me? I don't think we've met, have we?"

"Not quite. Though I am anxious to meet the man behind the stories. The Alliance hero who destroyed Cartaan's finest vessel and slaughtered its finest warriors. My people."

Dax's face sank. "Crap," he said to himself. "Look, funny you should bring that up—"

"Enough talk, Commander." Eyldwan's patience grew thin. "My men are on their way. You have until then to decide your fate and the fate of your companions."

The transmission ended, leaving the crew to contemplate. Sanders broke the silence.

"What are our options, Commander?"

"What options?" O'Reilly snapped back. "We give this phony up and be done with it."

"You actually think they'd let us go?"

"It's worth a shot, at least!"

Kiko joined in. "You can't do that to Dax!"

"He did it to himself! And we have to get dragged into it with him?"

The bickering continued as Logan stood silently wrestling with her own thoughts. Dax kept his eyes on her as she ever so slightly began to raise her pistol.

"Stop!"

Everyone did, turning toward the shout. Toward Dax.

"I'll go," he said casually, much to everyone's shock.

"Sir?"

"It's all right, Sanders. I'll go. Hey, we got nowhere to run, and they'll kill us all anyway, right? At least this way, maybe I can give you guys a shot at getting out of here." He turned back to Logan. "Right?"

She paused, in disbelief of the first genuine moment between them. She saw no deception in his eyes. He was going to hand himself over to the enemy, and he willingly came to that decision seconds before she was about to force him. It wasn't right, and she chastised herself for even considering the option. But Dax wasn't wrong. There were no alternatives. She nodded to him solemnly. "Right."

Kiko remained at Dax's arm. He pried her grip loose and she relented. "But . . ."

Dern, looking as though he was caught in a highly uncomfortable family meeting, glanced back to his instruments. "Looks like they launched a shuttle. Should be here in a few minutes."

Dax walked Kiko over to her uncle. "You should get everyone into the bunks at the far end. Lock everything down just in case they do a sweep. I'll meet them out here."

Dern waved the crew over. "This way, everybody."

Logan hung back a moment as the rest slowly headed into the station. "Harrison, I—" He looked at her, but she couldn't find any words to say. She managed a sincere "Good luck." Dax gave an appreciative nod, and she made her way back to the rest of the group. As she neared the bulkhead door, Kiko ran past her back toward Dax.

"Hey!"

Dax sighed at her. "Kid, come on. These guys are coming. You gotta get going."

"So, you *are* Dax, right?"

"Yeah, kid. It's just, it's complicated."

"So . . . you got a plan, right?"

He looked down at the hopeful doe-eyed girl. "Me?" He scoffed and smirked at her. "Of course I do."

Reassured, she smiled back and ran off to join the others. As expected, the approaching shuttle touched down within a few short minutes. Immediately, the main ramp began to lower, and Dax raised his hands in surrender. He closed his eyes a moment to find his calm, competing against the growing marching of boots in his ears. When he opened them, he was fully surrounded by a handful of Eyldwan's mercenaries, all with rifles drawn at his head. Mostly Carteagan, a couple Darshyll, and Khern emerging last. He towered over Dax and leaned in face-to-face, a bit too close for comfort. Dax smelled what he could only silently describe to himself as halitosis from hell. He kept his composure, however, and even managed a smile. He was screwed anyway. *Might as well put on the show*, he thought.

"Umm . . . take me to your leader." They obliged him with an ardent shove toward the shuttle. Minutes later, they were en route back toward the warship, Dax sitting cuffed with guards at both sides. Khern stood behind the pilot, speaking into a communicator.

"We are clear, *saakesh*. Fire when ready."

"What?!" Dax jumped to his feet, but the guards immediately knocked him back to his seat.

On the warship, a gunner targeted the station on his screens. "Primary cannon charging," he growled. Eyldwan watched stoically from his captain's chair.

In the shuttle, Dax struggled at his shackles to no avail. With nowhere for him to go, he noticed his captors had grown lax, turning their backs and laughing over their victory. Not that it mattered. What could he do?

Then he remembered his comms pin. They didn't take it! He adjusted his shackled hands and tapped it as discreetly as possible. "Kid," he whispered. "Kid, you copy? Come on, I know you got one of these things."

Kiko sat huddled in the comms station bunk when she heard the communicator in her pocket. She moved to a quiet corner, away from the rest of the group before pulling it out excitedly. "Dax!"

She came through the other end a little too loud. Dax loudly cleared his throat in a poor attempt to cover. His captors glanced over, saw him smiling back at them, and thankfully turned away in annoyance. "Keep it down, kid," he whispered back.

"Sorry."

"Listen, get #7 and take it to SAMM."

"But you said not to—"

"I know what I said. Forget what I said. You gotta use #7 now! Take it to SAMM and—"

A powerful hand grabbed Dax, pulling him up and holding him against the shuttle wall. "What is this?!" The guard grabbed the comms pin and threw it to the floor.

Dax shouted desperately at the communicator. "Take it to SAMM! He'll know what to do!" *CRUNCH!* A heavy boot smashed the pin into oblivion.

Kiko knew she had to get to her workshop. She knew she had to act fast, and she knew no sensible adult would let her leave that bunk. She searched her pockets and produced a small screwdriver. As nonchalant as she could be, she wandered over toward a small fuse box against the wall. With no one paying attention, she pried the cover off and yanked on the wires inside. A quick spark later and the overhead lights blacked out. Logan readied her pistol, Sanders yelped, O'Reilly and Dern exchanged "What the hell?" comments, and Kiko was out the door with no one the wiser.

The eleven-year-old sprinted like a bat out of hell, nearly tripping and tumbling down to her workshop. It was already clear she wouldn't be able to carry the heavy piece of machinery to the *Crichton*. She dove toward the hovercart, throwing the contents off to make room, then dropped the #7 hyperdrive on it with a slam. Without missing a beat, she was on her way back up, the cart gliding up the stairway with ease.

She had almost made it to the docking bay when the first blasts hit. The warship's primary cannon fired and decimated a quarter of the entire station, dangerously close to the bunk areas. The crew were thrown about. Kiko screamed, falling to her hands and knees at the entrance to the dock. The hovercart flew ahead of her until it slammed against the side of the *Crichton*. She got to her feet and kept running.

Eyldwan directed his gunner. "Fire until there is nothing left." A second wave destroyed nearly another quarter of the station, completely detaching a large section, which reeled off into space.

The crew held on to whatever they could as the gravity fluxes, blaring alarms, and blackouts disoriented them all. Thankfully, the auto-sealing systems remained intact, instantly shielding the breaches that would have otherwise sucked everyone and everything out into nothingness. Kiko, now in the *Crichton*'s engine room, sat in a sea of wires and engine grease.

SAMM quickly guided her through rigging the experimental hardware to the ship, but not without multiple nagging interludes. "I must again advise caution, young miss. This is not a tested addition to the ship's systems. You may be in danger of—"

"Just tell me what to do next!"

"Last connections: red conduit to green port. Twist them together, and please hold on to something!"

Kiko fell back, startled as the hyperdrive glowed with a brilliant light. She smiled excitedly, until she began to see smoke and a spark from the surrounding circuitry. She ran for cover.

Eyldwan watched as the hyperdrive energy encased the entire comms station, the light blinding his gunner through his targeting visor. "Continue fire, now!" He did so, but it was too late. Comms Relay Station 742 (what was left of it) vanished, leaving Eyldwan to glare at the empty black of space.

CHAPTER 10

DAX DIDN'T REFLECT on his life choices very often, but it wasn't every day he found himself held captive on a Carteagan warship. He presumed he'd be dead soon, and he found that such a revelation tended to make the mind wander. He thought about . . . Well, to be fair, he didn't have many deep thoughts. Mostly it was things he would've liked to enjoy again before the end. Marisa's spectacular long legs, the best beer he ever had, and a plate of carne asada fries. Good Mexican food was hard to come by these days, but he swore he'd track some down if he ever made it out of this mess.

To his own surprise, Dax eventually thought of Logan. Then Sanders and Kiko, and to a lesser degree O'Reilly and Dern. Really, the latter two were simply out of association, but the rest Dax figured for decent people. He hoped they had all made it out alive. His captors didn't say otherwise, but he assumed there was hope judging from the rage on their faces when he came aboard. Or maybe Carteagans just always looked like that.

He still couldn't believe he'd volunteered himself for surrender. He was still processing what possessed him to do that, no matter how decent his recent companions were. Maybe it was a bit of penance on his part. Maybe it had something to do with the fact that despite all his fans, in reality his best and only friend was an artificial intelligence programmed to like him. He knew what SAMM would say to that. "Programmed to assist, not to like."

A giant belch from the center of the room snapped Dax's meandering brain back to reality. He was in the medical bay, restrained against some industrial piping along the wall. The owner of the belch stood at a workbench, meticulously setting out a particularly scary-looking series of knives. Dax wondered if he was doing so purposely in his view.

"So, I take it you're the doctor on board?"

"Unofficial surgeon is more like it," the creature answered. The voice was gruff and the accent was strange. Dax thought it almost sounded like a British gangster. He got a better look as the figure picked up one of the knives and began walking toward him. Not Carteagan, Darshyll, or even Verdasian. It was quite human, but the proportions were off. The features exaggerated. Dax noted a very orange hue in the skin, like an artificial tan gone overboard.

"You're . . . you're . . . I'm sorry, but what the hell are you?"

"Indulan!" he shouted back. "You Alliance types. Always thinking you've seen it all." Dax wasn't familiar with the species, but he immediately wondered if they were all as seemingly short and overweight as this one. As the Indulan was currently brandishing a blade around, he of course wondered this silently.

"Look, I was trying to tell your boss back there: I'm not exactly the conquering hero you're looking for so—*ahh!*" The Indulan drove the tip of the knife into Dax's left shoulder. He cried out as the blade twisted out a small electronic device from under the skin.

Dax howled in pain again as the knife came out. The Indulan stared at the object a moment. Small and circular, like a quarter. "Always liked these Alliance trackers. Easy to pop out." He grinned at Dax. "Although sometimes making a mess is fun."

Dax breathed through the terrible burning in his arm as his captor dropped the tracker on the bench and smashed it with the butt of the knife handle. The medical bay door slid open and Dax looked up to see Eyldwan and Khern walking in. "Oh yay, now it's a party," he said miserably to himself.

Eyldwan turned to the Indulan. "Is it done?"

"All clear, Captain. His friends won't be coming for him anytime soon."

"Well done, Xihgat."

Zig-what? Dax thought. *What's with these guys and the names?*

Eyldwan approached with an almost polite demeanor. "Commander, it is an honor to finally meet you."

"Yeah, I'm having a great time. I should stop by more often."

Dax could have sworn he almost charmed a smile out of the former general. The former-general-turned-war-criminal-fugitive-psychopath who was holding him captive, that is.

"I'll get right to it, Commander. The only reason you are still alive is because I'd prefer that you witness the fall of your homeworld. I watched my comrades burn above Feron. Why should you be denied the same courtesy?"

Dax hung his head in exasperation. He knew they wouldn't believe him, but he had to try. "I'm telling you people, you got the wrong guy."

"Really?" Eyldwan kneeled down close to Dax, studying his face. "The Hero of the Alliance. The man who turned the tide of war. I've been in prison, and I still find it difficult to escape *your* face."

His coal-black eyes burned into Dax's, causing him to stutter. "No, really. I—I know how it sounds, but it's all a fake.

I'm a fake! The stories, the victories, the battles . . . It was made up to get people to enlist! I'm a poster!" He could see Eyldwan wasn't buying it. He carried on desperately. "I mean, do I look like some kind of warrior to you?!"

"So tell me, whoever you are." Eyldwan's measured tone grew venomous. "Who destroyed the *Akshataa* in the ring of Feron?"

"Ak—Ak what?"

"The ship! The ship with my men, the finest servants of the empire!"

Dax panicked. "Oh . . . Well, that . . . Okay, that, in all honesty, that one was me. But it was a complete accident. I swear!"

Eyldwan held up a dismissive claw and got up to leave. "No deception or foolish heroics will stand in our way, Commander. You shall remain on board until our task is done."

Dax perked up. "And . . . and then I can leave?"

"Of course." Eyldwan looked back with a smile. "Nearest airlock, quick as we can."

Somewhere in space, the remnants of Comms Relay Station 742 floated adrift, its stabilizing systems (along with a thousand other things) destroyed. Sanders and his stomach were immensely thankful that at least the artificial gravity seemed intact, as he and the rest of the crew dizzily found their footing.

Logan was the first to ask the million-credit question. "What the hell was that?"

"We jumped," Dern said, though he couldn't believe the answer himself.

Neither could Sanders. "How's that possible?"

Everyone turned as the door opened, and Kiko stood triumphantly behind it, looking like a cartoon character that had been caught in an explosion. She smiled back at the crew as engine grease dripped from her fingers and a wild tuft of singed hair smoked off the side of her head. Her smile faded as she saw their expressions. "What?"

Xihgat sat at his workbench, a pair of smart goggles strapped to his head. On the bench in front of him was a large glass jar full of murky yellow liquid. As Dax squinted, he was able to catch glimpses of a small mantis-like alien swimming around inside. Whatever it was, it sent a chill down his spine. With a large pair of tweezers, Xihgat fished the creature out and pinned it to the bench. It let out a defiant screech and attempted to wriggle free as the goggles began analyzing. Xihgat grunted as the computer tracked its movement, pulse, and respiration, but ultimately failed to identify the species.

I know how that feels, pal, Dax thought to the downtrodden creature. Despite the messy events a few hours earlier, Dax had mostly settled into his captivity for the time being. His wrists were rubbed raw from several prior attempts to squeeze out of his restraints. His restraints, which he noted, were some well-worn ropes. As though he were being held captive by pirates. How absurd. All this fancy tech on this damn ship and they couldn't spring for some slightly more comfortable mag-cuffs? Or better yet, a shielded cell where he could at least move around freely with no threat of escape? Regardless, after breaking loose proved pointless, his biggest battle wasn't against fear or panic. It was boredom. Sheer, soul-crushing boredom. And boredom was winning. At least Xihgat remained on watch for the bulk of the time. Dax was still trying to get a read on him, which made for a good distraction. He wasn't a mercenary. Not enough of an ex-military-looking-to-keep-killing-things vibe. Not a typical nutjob terrorist, either. Too casual. Not that Dax was planning on having a beer with him or anything.

"You know, for an alien I don't recognize, you sound almost Earther. What's the story?"

"I'm well traveled," he said, absolutely not interested in conversation. He readied a surgical scalpel in his hand, coordinating with the goggle displays targeting the test subject's nervous system.

"Who's your friend there?"

"Quiet."

"New pet?"

With Dax distracting him, Xihgat sliced into the creature too deep and off target. It let out a final squeal and fell limp. "Experiment. Maybe I'll do the same with you if you don't keep quiet."

"You know, torturing small animals is a sign of homicidal tendencies. I'm no professional, but you should probably talk to someone." Xihgat ignored him and carried on his work. He scraped the remains into a tray on the far side of the workbench. A button press later and a laser field instantly burned the fresh carcass out of existence. He turned to a shelf along the wall, lined with a series of similar creature-filled jars. More test subjects. As he selected a suitable replacement, Dax began to fidget. He was exhausted. Everything ached from sitting against the hard wall and floor. The open wound in his shoulder ached worse. He shifted his seat, attempting to adjust, but nothing helped.

"Excuse me, Mr. Zagnut? You at least have some tequila or something to pour on this, right? I mean, if I die from some horrible infection, I don't think your boss will appreciate that. He doesn't seem like the forgiving type."

Xihgat dropped his tools with a frustrated groan and stared at Dax, who smiled back.

"Come on, I even have a bottle of some Darshyll stuff in my jacket here. Top-shelf. Can't even pronounce the name, but I've been saving it." Dax figured he would carry on until his charm won Xihgat over, or Xihgat killed him. "It's a little memento from this pretty hairy bar fight a few years back. Apparently I made eyes with the wrong colonist's wife—completely honest mistake—and ended up scrapping with her giant of a husband." Dax chuckled. "Man, he was not happy with me."

He thought he might have rambled for too long, but then Xihgat got up and pulled a tall bottle from a personal locker nearby. "Fine, if it'll stop your blubbering." He uncorked the bottle and poured a small portion of the liquid on the wound. Dax tensed up from the initial sting, then relaxed as the burning subsided and the numbing effect kicked in. Whatever it was, it was potent stuff.

"Ahh, thank you." Suddenly, Xihgat shifted his aim and poured the rest of the bottle on Dax's head with a grin. Dax protested between coughs and spitting as the concoction went everywhere.

"Ack!" *Cough.* "Come on, really? In the eyes too?" He calmed after a moment as the taste set on his tongue. "Hey, that's actually not bad."

Xihgat, annoyed as hell, punched Dax hard across the jaw. "Shut. Your. Mouth!" He pulled a large hunting knife from his belt, brandishing it close in front of Dax's face. This was a surgical tool of a much different sort. "Or keep it up," he continued. "And I'll cut that silver tongue of yours right out. The captain said to keep you alive. He didn't say undamaged."

Dax got the message, loud and clear.

Just as the confrontation appeared to be over, Xihgat turned back, digging out the miniature bottle from Dax's jacket pocket. "Top-shelf, huh? Much obliged." He grinned and walked back to his workbench.

CHAPTER 11

"YOU HAVE GOT to be joking." O'Reilly rubbed his brow in frustration. "I cannot believe we're going through this again. No, actually, I can believe it. I'm just choosing not to accept it."

While Dern and Kiko spent the last few hours getting the *Crichton* running again, O'Reilly had locked himself away in one of the bunks, pretending to rest. He was in fact avoiding the crusading Sanders, who had been ceaselessly petitioning the crew to mount a rescue operation for the kidnapped commander.

Now, however, with Logan's aid, he had corralled everyone into the *Crichton*'s common room to weigh their options.

"We have to go back for him," Sanders repeated. "There is no other option."

"Look, I'm proud of you for showing some backbone for once, but in case you haven't been keeping count, we made it out of certain death twice today. And you want go for thirds? For that smug son of a—"

"We wouldn't even be here if Dax didn't give himself up and have Kiko jump us out of there!" Sanders fired back, cutting the doctor off.

Kiko joined in with a "Yeah!"

"Good! So he finally did something honorable. Let's not waste it."

"All right, enough!" Everyone shut up as Logan took charge of the room. She knew the call she had to make. She didn't like it herself, but the situation was clear. Central Station was still a long way off by several star systems. With the relay trashed, there would be no contacting the fleet. She also knew in her gut what was right. She knew what her father would have done. "We have to find him."

O'Reilly's face dropped. "Oh, not you too. Weaver, you wanted him gone more than anybody. You said it yourself; he's a fraud! We don't know *who* the hell he is!"

"He gave himself up for us, and I let him."

"What, so you feel guilty? He made the call."

"A second before me," she confessed. "I was going to give him up, and if he resisted, I would've forced him to do it. Now what kind of officer does that make me?"

"One that lives to fight another day," Dern said under his breath.

Sanders snapped back. "By sacrificing one of our own?!"

"Easy, Boy Scout. It was a joke."

"Whether or not Harrison is the man we were expecting him to be," Logan continued, "he is a commander of the Alliance navy. Not to mention, that rank includes access to sensitive information. Defense codes, base locations."

O'Reilly shook his head. "Wait a minute. With this deal he has with the Alliance, I'm assuming his rank is honorary. He probably doesn't know a damn thing."

"We can't take that chance."

"This is absolutely insane. We should get the ship running and get our asses back to Central as fast as we—"

"Let me make this perfectly clear!" Logan had had enough of the old doctor's complaints, and while she was addressing the room, she made a point to deliver her message to his face. "We have an enemy who just openly attacked military personnel and civilians. They have stolen Alliance tech, which command doesn't want to tell us about, so I'd guess it's a weapon. Not to mention they've kidnapped the pain in the ass that I've been made personally responsible for."

She addressed them with the presence of a drill instructor staring down a fresh batch of recruits. It worked. "Now we are cut off from the fleet, which means the only thing on this side of the galaxy left to stop that ship . . . is us." The room fell silent as the grim prospect sank in. The tension hanging in the air was thick enough to cut with a knife. In fact, it may have necessitated a chainsaw.

"And people ask why I didn't sign up," Dern quipped.

Logan turned back to the group. "And yes, Harrison *did* save us back there. And whether he knows anything or not, the Carteagans will think he does, and they'll do anything to get it out of him."

"We can't leave him like that," Sanders reaffirmed.

Kiko's eyes bugged. After a brief silence, she asked the obvious question. "So, what do we do?"

Logan's communicator chirped. "Lieutenant," SAMM said. "I have located the commander."

Minutes later, the crew was gathered on the bridge. SAMM displayed a star map on the main console, tracking Dax's personal locator signal. "It appears the commander's personal locator has stopped in orbit of Delphine."

"Delphine?" Sanders perked up. "I know where that is. It's a gas giant, right? That's not far at all."

O'Reilly stared at him. "Have you been there?"

"No, I memorized star charts in the academy. I mean, I know it's not required because the fleet ships keep their charting software regularly updated, but I just thought it might be good to know any—"

"Sanders," Logan stopped him. "We got it, thanks. Anyway, it's still plenty far off from any Alliance-controlled system." She mentally ruled out the chance for local reinforcements.

SAMM's displays flickered. "My apologies for the delay. To prevent further damage, my systems were forced into low-power mode after the hyperspace jump overloaded—"

"Yeah, yeah, shut up. You're forgiven." Dern rubbed his eyes.

"If we're going to act, we have to move now."

"And do what, Lieutenant?" Dern looked around as the crew stared back. "Look, I'm no soldier, but what do you people think you're gonna do? Just go knock on the door? Take them on yourselves?"

"If we can find a way aboard, a small team could stand a chance if we move fast." Logan had seen action like this before. Small-team infiltration and extraction. Granted, her team had not previously consisted of an aging medical chief and his assistant.

Sanders took a step forward. "I've had plenty of sim combat training. I can handle myself."

"Sims aren't the same as a real firefight, boy," O'Reilly shot back.

"What other choice do we have?"

Dern sighed, folding his arms across his chest. "And me and my niece, I hope you didn't plan on us joining in this suicide run?" He looked to Logan, but she knew there was no easy answer.

"I can't recommend you stay here. We're lucky this place hasn't collapsed on our heads already, and Utynai could still be targeting comms stations."

"So stay here and die or come for the ride and die. Nice to have options."

Kiko excitedly tapped Logan's sleeve. "Oh! We can hide in the engine room. Seal the bulkhead door, and there's no way they're getting in there. We can keep those engines running smooth for you too." She looked up to see her uncle staring down at her with a raised eyebrow. "What?"

Logan looked to Dern, and he confirmed the plan with another heavy sigh followed by an apprehensive nod. Kiko was all smiles. Sanders nodded the go-ahead as well. "Doctor? I'm going to need every hand I can get."

In their time together, the crew had witnessed Dan O'Reilly's ability to produce some of the most profoundly intense frowns in the galaxy. In this moment, he may have bested all his previous works to date. "You're all mad. Bunch of *faakesh'tac* idiots . . . But since I don't have another way out of here, and you'll probably all be in need of medical attention soon, I suppose I'm in."

Logan smiled. "Good. Now just how much Cardic do you speak, exactly?"

"Well, I'm a little rusty these days, but I suppose I can hold a conver—" He paused, a wave of dread striking his face. "Why?"

Eyldwan paced along the bridge, his already near-nonexistent patience wearing thinner by the second. "How much longer must we wait?"

A timid human man, an Alliance scientist, stood nearby, sweating bullets. Under his shortly trimmed hair, a spot of dry blood was visible on his scalp. A memento from his kidnapping at the hands of Eyldwan's forces. He removed his glasses with a shaky hand to wipe them down. "We are having difficulty with the device's output. A large amount of power is required to—"

Eyldwan marched up to him. "You claimed to know this technology. That you could enhance it to meet my needs."

"And that is precisely what I'm attempting to do. By converting the gases from Delphine's atmosphere into a power source, you could achieve the output you desire, but it's volatile." As the poor scientist continued his nervous rambling, the Carteagans' ruthless eyes showed no interest in explanations. Eyldwan gripped the scientist's face across the jaw with a large green hand. His pointed nails pressed into his cheek.

"Work quickly. We are exposed here."

"Th-there may be another solution," he stuttered through Eyldwan's grip. As Eyldwan released him to explain, a proximity alert stole his attention.

Another of the escaped convicts, now acting as an operations tech, studied his monitoring screen. "*Saakesh!* Vessel approaching from long range. Alliance signature." The long-range scanners identified the now familiar ship. "It's the *Crichton!*" He relayed the image to the bridge's main viewscreen.

Eyldwan stared at it in disbelief. He scoffed. "What is this? Arm the forward batteries and prepare—"

"Sir, they are hailing us." The ops tech, Kriivak, tapped his controls, activating the intercom.

A voice came over the transmission. Gruff and commanding, and with only a few words carefully sounded out, the translation roughly came out to this: "To the brave guardians of the empire, please acknowledge. Repeat, to the guardians of the one true Cartaan, acknowledge."

"This is *Saakesh* Utynai in command of this warship. Identify yourself."

"I am Da'jek Tahg of the Kreshak Province, where your loyal are still many, General. I wish to join your campaign."

Eyldwan narrowed his gaze, pausing in thought for a moment. "How interesting to find a brother of Cartaan so far from home, and in that Alliance vessel."

On the bridge of the *Crichton*, O'Reilly sat at the comms console as Logan stood nearby for support. He did not look happy. "I . . . followed you after your victory on Vega. You were pursuing this vessel, yes? I have eliminated the crew. Some survivors I have held for interrogation. I bring them and their ship to you as a . . . toy . . . As a gift!" He winced at the mistake, slapping his hand over his eyes.

Eyldwan again paused, debating his next move. "Well done, Da'jek Tahg. Continue your approach and dock. I will meet with you shortly." He cut the transmission and turned to Khern. "Have your men down there and ready in force." Grabbing the beleaguered scientist by the arm, Eyldwan led him forcefully out of the room. "Tell me of this alternate solution."

O'Reilly slumped back in his seat, relieved the encounter was over. "All right, genius. Now what? That is, if you think they actually bought that."

"Probably not," Logan said. "But he's curious enough to let us on the ship, which is all we need."

"You know, as much as it pains me to give him credit, I think Harrison might actually be the sanest of you bunch. At least he knows when to run for it."

The *Crichton* steadily sailed toward the ominous warship. Sanders steeled his nerves as a rumbling signaled that they were now being pulled in by a tractor beam. He took a long calming breath and reminded himself why he was there in the first place. Four years in the academy. Denied training. Being told he didn't pass the physical requirements for combat. Nearly scrubbing out until he decided not to quit. Commander Harrison wouldn't quit. He began medic training instead, befriended the sim technicians, and eventually convinced them to allow him access after hours. He learned everything he could in hopes that soon he would be able to petition the board for another shot.

The commander may not have been everything he had hoped, but it was the commander who gave a young Alex Sanders the drive he needed to keep fighting. It was the commander who gave himself to the enemy to save him. And now it was the commander who needed his help. It was quite an impressive motivational speech Sanders gave himself in his head. Now if only he could stop this damned flop sweat.

"This way." Logan led him toward a weapons locker in the cargo bay. Dax didn't have much in stock beyond the Alliance standard issue. A single pulse pistol and a ZF-8 assault rifle, matching the set Logan had brought on board with her. She checked and loaded each weapon, giving Sanders a guided crash course on the basics. Thankfully, the training from the simulations came back to him fairly easily.

"Stay close to me," she continued. "Let me take point; check your corners and keep moving unless I say otherwise."

"Yes, ma'am."

Logan tapped her comms pin. "Mr. Dern, are you secure?"

Dern shut the heavy bulkhead door to the engine room. Kiko watched with fascination as the locking mechanisms went to work sealing them in. "We're good, Lieutenant. Locked tight, and we've bypassed the outer overrides. Try not to get shot up. You're our ride out of here."

"Copy that." Something caught Logan's eye as she switched off her comm. The upholstery lining the bottom of the weapons locker was pulled up ever so slightly in one corner. She pulled at the edge, revealing a false bottom and two concussion grenades lying in the space below. She sighed with relief at the extra firepower. "Thanks, Harrison."

Sanders struggled to hold up the shockingly heavy rifle. O'Reilly grabbed it with ease, handing him the pistol instead. "Here, try this. Give me that before you hurt yourself."

Logan watched as O'Reilly checked the weapon as though it were second nature. "Doc?"

"It was 'Gunnery Sergeant' before it was 'Doc,' Lieutenant, and you need the help. You don't have to worry about me."

"All right then."

As she moved into position at the cargo bay door, Sanders leaned in to whisper, "You never told me that."

For once, O'Reilly had no grouchy reply. No curmudgeonly comeback. Not even a passing surly remark. "It's not something I go around advertising."

Sanders stared at his mentor a moment. He thought he might have been mistaken, but O'Reilly seemed troubled. "Is everything all right?"

O'Reilly ignored him, joining Logan at the far side of the cargo bay. Sanders received the message. The conversation was over, for now. He shook it off and took some quick breaths, getting his head in the game before moving to the door.

CHAPTER 12

A SMALL GROUP of mercenaries stood with weapons at the ready as the *Crichton*'s cargo door slowly lowered. All interior lights were shut off as they stared ahead into total darkness.

The Carteagan at the head of the pack stepped forward. "Show yourself!" Out of the black, a small object flew toward the leader, landing at his boots. He looked down to see a steel cylinder with a rapidly beeping and flashing red light. "Grenade!" The single word barely escaped his maw before the concussive blast sent him and several others flying. As the blast smoke provided cover, Logan, Sanders, and O'Reilly emerged from the *Crichton*, running and gunning. Logan and O'Reilly swiftly took out the few stragglers still standing. As the commotion died down and the smoke cleared, Sanders took stock of the action.

"Did . . . did I get any?"

As a red alert sounded off through the bridge, Kriivak looked to his screens. "Explosion in the docking bay, sir! Three humans from the Alliance ship advancing!"

Khern pushed him out of the way of the controls and opened a comms channel. "Reinforcements to the docking bay now!"

Xihgat and Dax both looked up toward the door as muffled gunfire echoed through the ship's hallways. Xihgat tapped a screen on the wall and called up a security feed. Witnessing three gunmen in Alliance gear advancing through the ship, he dropped his tools. "Oh, the hell with this."

Dax watched curiously as Xihgat bumbled around the room in a panic, packing a suitcase with whatever important items he deemed necessary. "Hey! Zagnut, what's going on? Hello?"

"Looks like this job is off," he said, briefly stopping only as he banged his shin into his workbench stool. "I didn't sign up for combat."

"What the . . ." Dax was speechless. All that big, bad posturing. All that scary knife-waving and tongue-slicing talk, and now he was showing his true colors. Dax couldn't believe he had met someone more clueless and cowardly than himself. Then he realized what he thought of himself at that moment, and he wasn't sure whether to laugh or be offended. "Are you telling me you joined Eyelid's revolution and *didn't* expect a fight?!"

"I'm not one of these zealots, ready to die for glory." He laughed at the notion. "Strictly research, pay on delivery. Oh, he's got plans for your lot."

"What do you mean? What plans?" Xihgat ignored him, continuing to pack in a rush. He collected his specimen jars from the nearby shelf, dropping one as he again banged into the stool. The jar shattered onto the ground, and the Darshyll liquor bottle fell from the workbench with a clang. Xihgat angrily grabbed the stool, now his mortal enemy, and heaved it across the room.

"Come on! What plans? I'll double whatever he's paying you!"

"Nice try, Commander. But the Alliance can still kiss my *doungas.*" He sealed the suitcase and headed to the door. "Been a pleasure."

"Well, at least cut me loose!" Dax struggled with his restraints as Xihgat disappeared out the door. His heart sank. *I guess it's all over now,* he thought. Xihgat was his last hope, and now he was gone just as Dax felt they were building a rapport of sorts. He figured he'd soon be dead, either by the hands of his captors or whoever the hell was raiding the ship. He pondered for a moment whether he might end up in better hands with whoever that may be. Perhaps they were bad guys of the slightly less bad variety. The Vastra Prime Warlords, for example. Being held hostage by an outlaw hovercycle gang could be fun. Sure, they were known gun smugglers, but they were mostly just out for a good time. Fewer body counts and more gentlemanly barroom brawls. Hell, with enough time, they might even make him an honorary member.

In the midst of Dax contemplating his potential tattooed, headband-wearing future, his eyes fell on the broken glass jar on the ground. He rolled his eyes at his own density, then began making a move for the shards. The ropes still had him pinned to the wall, so he twisted awkwardly toward the floor, stretching a leg ahead toward the glass.

Logan, Sanders, and O'Reilly moved quickly down the main corridor. Sanders kept his eyes on a portable tracker attached to his forearm, homing in on the commander's location. Logan pressed on, but silently noted how massive the enemy ship was. Perhaps she had truly bitten off more than she could chew. She choked the thought down immediately before it could shake her confidence. There was no time for that now. "Which way, Sanders?"

"Um, about twenty meters northwest." They rounded a corner only to be met by two Carteagan mercs running in their direction. The trio dove behind a nearby stack of cargo bins, barely dodging the hail of bullets.

Dax stretched and strained enough that he thought he may end up with a hernia, but finally he managed to land the tip of his boot on the glass shard closest to him. He carefully dragged it toward his hands and began cutting away, laughing, exasperated and half-delirious. His celebration was cut short as he heard a bizarre chittering sound. What the hell? He looked around the medical bay. Nothing. Seconds later, he heard it again and locked eyes with the shattered jar remains. The specimen inside was still alive. Another mantis-like creature, similar to the previously dissected one, began stirring from the shards. "Ewww." Dax watched as the thing clawed at the air, trying to right itself. He cut at his ropes faster.

Shots continued echoing through the hall outside. Dax again wondered what he'd be stepping into. Maybe he could slip away during the commotion, find a docking bay and hopefully a transport off the ship. At this moment, however, all he really wanted was out of this room. The creepy alien mantis bug had righted itself, and Dax could swear it was giving him a nasty look. It also appeared about twice as big as its dead friend. As he made the final cut, the creature let out a screech and charged toward him. A cowardly yelp later, Dax jumped to his feet and ran for the door, scooping up his fallen liquor bottle along the way.

The med bay door opened, and Dax ran out to freedom mere steps behind the mercs embroiled in the shootout. He turned on his heel back into the med bay as one of them spotted him and fired in his direction.

"Harrison!" Logan called out from down the hall, but it was too late. "Dammit!"

Dax quickly eyed the room for an alternate exit. An oversized air vent on the far wall looked promising. He dragged Xihgat's workbench over, kicking away the alien bug as it gnawed at his pant leg. "Gah! You slimy piece of— Get off!" He kicked it back far enough to escape, then climbed onto the bench. Thankfully, the vent cover slid off with ease, and he crawled headfirst into the darkness.

Dax had never found himself susceptible to claustrophobia, but that didn't mean scooting along the cramped ventilation system was in any way pleasant. The air was thick and humid, much like the air throughout the rest of the ship, meant to mimic Cartaan's atmosphere. The effect was even more concentrated in the vent, however, and Dax felt as though breathing was an actual physical struggle. Yet there was light at the end of the tunnel. Literally, a faint light poured in from a connected room ahead. He crawled as quickly as he could across the shaft until he began to hear voices coming from the room. He made a dead stop, terrified that he would have been heard. He waited a few moments, expecting shouts, whispers, open gunfire. But nothing happened. He was safe for now, and he carefully crept ahead to peek through the vent.

The grating blocked most of his view, but Dax could make out a pair of bodies rushing around the room, shutting items away in storage containers. He assumed they were securing sensitive information should the hostile forces make their way to this part of the ship. The giant piece of tech sitting in the middle of the room furthered his assumption. Eyldwan and a timid human man stood over it as their conversation continued.

"This is your design?" Eyldwan caressed the machine. Clearly it was something important, probably a weapon, but Dax still couldn't place it. It didn't look like a nuke. A water heater? A snow cone maker? The human, seemingly a scientist or tech head of some sort, rambled on with technical specifics that Dax barely understood and Eyldwan did not seem impressed with. He pointed out his design schematic on a holo-projector. It appeared as though the device was meant to attach to something much larger. Dax wasn't able to glean much else before the holo was shut off.

"I need absolutes, not half-assurances. Will it work or not?"

The exasperated scientist sighed, trying his best to explain what he already had without angering his captor. "Like I said, the relay will allow you to achieve the desired yield without risking the overloads we experienced in the original design. It's a bit of a sloppy solution, but it will work as you wanted."

"You are sure then?"

"With one hundred percent certainty, yes."

"Good." Without missing a beat, Eyldwan pulled a pistol from his belt and shot the scientist in the head. Dax felt a jolt of shock and sickness surge through his entire body. He slapped his hand hard over his mouth, gripping it to hold back the reactionary shouts and gasps. He lay there for a moment, trembling in the vent, unable to take his eyes off the fallen man as Eyldwan casually continued. "Thank you for your assistance. Your services are no longer required."

Dax took another minute after Eyldwan left the room, allowing himself to catch his breath and calm the shock tremors running through him. The silence didn't last long, as he heard the familiar screech of the mantis creature echoing from behind him. "Oh shit." He started on the move again, scooting through the vent as fast as he could.

Back in the standoff, Logan gunned down the last merc, and the *Crichton* trio continued moving down the corridor of death. "Reload, catch your breaths, but stay alert. Sanders?"

He looked back at the tracker, perplexed. "He's on the move, Lieutenant." Was he looking at it upside down? "He's . . . all over the place. He should be right around here, I—I can't tell where he is."

"Well, find him." As Logan looked down to reload, O'Reilly spotted three more Carteagans rounding the corner ahead.

"Down!" They scrambled for cover against an alcove in the wall as the battle resumed. O'Reilly pulled back as his rifle jammed. "Dammit! We can't keep this up! Throw a grenade to cover us! We gotta pull back!"

Logan shouted back to him between shots. "It's the last one!"

"Just use the damn thing, Weaver!"

In the vents above, Dax reached a grating directly above the hallway. He couldn't believe who he saw down below. "Guys? Guys! Guys, I'm up here!" It was no use. There was no hearing him over the ongoing firefight. Dax, on the other hand, was treated to the spine-chilling screeches of the alien bug on the hunt. He turned to the passage behind him just in time to see it charging at his face. "Shit!"

The creature lunged at him. Dax barely managed to hold it off, gripping its talon-like front legs as it tried to slash at him. Preoccupied with the horrific pincers inching closer and closer, he didn't notice that the epic struggle had forced him directly on top of the vent grating, and it had begun to creak under the pressure. Feeling himself beginning to sink, his eye darted to a corner of the grating just as it gave way. Too late. He dropped through in a free fall to the floor, landing on top of the mantis creature and splattering it.

"Commander!" Sanders nearly leapt to him without thinking. Logan passed her rifle to O'Reilly as she and Sanders pulled Dax to safety. He groaned in pain and disgust. His arm was a wreck, his hip and back had taken the brunt of the fall, and he was spitting bits of splattered alien bug from his mouth. It went everywhere. The thing had exploded on him like a pressurized piñata of entrails.

Logan propped him up against the wall of the alcove. "Harrison, you good?"

"Yeah. Fantastic."

O'Reilly continued firing, but paused as he caught a whiff of the commander. "Why do you smell like a bar?!"

"I'll explain later."

"Here!" Logan handed over her pulse pistol.

"You got a plan to get out of here?"

"Yeah. Shoot anything that moves, and follow me."

"That'll do." The group continued firing as they retreated back down toward the docking bay.

Eyldwan returned to the bridge.

"*Saakesh!*" Kriivak turned to deliver his report, but he paused as he saw the general's face, fresh blood still dripping off it.

The delay annoyed Eyldwan. Kriivak was showing fear, and fear was weakness. "Speak! What is it?"

"They . . . they have retrieved the commander."

Eyldwan's rage boiled under his scales. "*Khern!*"

The lieutenant obediently came to his side. Eyldwan grabbed him by the collar, pulling him in close. "They are stealing my prize. Stop them." He released him, and Khern dashed out of the bridge without a word.

The crew rushed toward the *Crichton*, catching their breaths after the long sprint down the hallway. Logan tapped her comm. "SAMM, open the ship."

"Right away, Lieutenant." The cargo ramp began to lower, and Logan allowed herself a moment to breathe. She took account of the crew. Everyone intact. It was a miracle. She then noticed Dax, who was leaning over with his head between his legs. His shoulder was a bloody mess.

"Are you hit?"

"What? Oh, no, they pulled out my tracker."

"What?" O'Reilly exchanged confused looks with the others.

"But . . . but that's how we found you."

"Oh, good." Dax smiled to Sanders. "That means the backup's working."

"Backup?"

"Yeah. Come on, Doc, you were there for the war. Carteagans found all the usual hiding spots. Shoulders, hips, palm of the hand. So I had a secondary put in just in case. Somewhere they'd never find it."

"Where?"

Dax almost replied but held back a moment, glancing downward toward his crotch, then shrugging back to Logan. "I'd rather not say."

The cargo ramp finished lowering just as two more of Eyldwan's mercs emerged from the corridor, blasting away. The collective *Crichton* crew all fired back, putting the attackers down quickly.

"All right, we're out of here!" O'Reilly knew their luck was bound to run out soon.

"Hey, Doc, wait a sec." With their attention turned back toward the docking bay wall, an interesting piece of tech caught

Dax's eye. "You speak the language, right? Is that as important as I think it is?"

O'Reilly examined the series of pulsing lights and tubing producing a small hum against the wall. A line of Cardic text ran directly above it. "Uh, energy . . . Generator . . . Tract . . . Yep, tractor beam."

"You got the big gun. Do you mind?"

"With pleasure." O'Reilly lifted the rifle and blasted at the generator until a small burst of sparks signaled its demise. The lights went dark and the humming ceased.

"Woo hoo!" Sanders smiled with glee. "Hey, you know, we're actually doing really good! I mean, I know it's dangerous and everything, and I've been trying to stay focused and all, but this is incredible! We're winning! I mean, we might be able to end this thing right here! Right?"

BAM! A single shot echoed against the docking bay walls as Sanders's body jerked. Everyone watched as he looked down in a daze and saw the blood coming from his lower torso.

Khern kneeled in a sniping position on the second-floor walkway above the docking bay, smoking gun in hand.

"Sanders!" O'Reilly leapt into action, pulling the young corporal into the cover of the ship as he fell to the ground. Logan traded shots with Khern, forcing him to take cover on the walkway. Dax and O'Reilly dragged Sanders up the ramp into the ship. The doctor began checking the wound. Dax's eyes darted frantically between Sanders's agony-stricken face and the hole in his abdomen.

"What—what do I do? What should I do? Doc, do I—"

"Shut up and hold him steady!" O'Reilly looked back to Sanders. "We gotta move you. It's going to hurt. Stay with me, all right?" They tried moving him farther, but could only get a couple feet more before his cries of agony made them stop.

O'Reilly kept pressure on the wound as Dax stared at the grim scene playing out. He looked back to Logan, still locked in the firefight, using the edge of the ship as cover. It was then he noticed the grenade clipped to her belt. He visibly shook the haze of shock out of his head. Something inside him replaced it. He wasn't sure if it was rage, or guilt, or something else entirely, but it possessed him. He walked back down the cargo ramp.

He grabbed the grenade and activated it, walking right past Logan and out into the open.

"Harrison!"

Dax quickly eyed the walkway. One second.

Khern revealed himself from his cover, lining up his shot. Two seconds.

Dax wound up and hurled the grenade. Khern's clear shot at Dax's heart was replaced by the beeping cylinder of metal rapidly approaching his face.

BOOM! Khern disappeared in the explosion of fire and smoke, but Dax and Logan witnessed enough to know he wasn't coming back. A section of the walkway supports buckled and collapsed, adding to the cacophony. Then silence. Logan watched in disbelief as Dax stared at the flaming wreckage. For a moment, just a moment, it was as though she saw the Commander Harrison from the stories. Without a word, he moved back to the ship, back to O'Reilly and Sanders. She followed as she spoke into her comm. "SAMM, fire up the engines."

"Starting engine sequence now."

"Dern, any extra push you can give us would be a help."

"Way ahead of you, Weaver." In the engine room, Dern closed a panel full of electronics on the side of the engine, wiping the sweat from his brow. "That should cut the lightdrive charge in half."

Kiko annoyingly tapped his shoulder. "They all made it, right? They found Dax?"

"I don't know! Go strap in. We're jumping."

The *Crichton* soared out of the warship at full speed. The forward cannons fired on them, but the small ship maneuvered away with ease. Within seconds, they disappeared from the sky with the accompanying lightspeed flash.

Eyldwan sat in his captain's chair as Ertac paced around him on the bridge. "The commander has escaped, and half your forces are dead, including your first officer. The Indulan has fled. It appears his shuttle launched during the fight without detection. And this supposed superweapon is a failure." He came to a stop directly in front of Eyldwan. "This campaign is over."

Eyldwan stroked his face, wiping the blood on the arm of his chair. "No. Not all is lost. The Alliance scientist left us a parting gift before I terminated his services. Set a course for the Sol System."

Ertac remained still, grimacing. The Darshyll giant was losing faith in the reputed legendarily ruthless general of Cartaan, and the casual attitude amid their losses was not helping. He wanted answers.

Eyldwan rose from his seat and repeated himself with an authoritarian growl. "Set a course for the Sol System."

CHAPTER 13

SANDERS LAY UNCONSCIOUS on the operating table as O'Reilly finished closing and cleaning up his wound. Tissue re-gens would repair a substantial amount of the muscle fibers, but he had some recovery ahead of him. He slowly opened his eyes, awaking with a wheeze and a coughing fit. The doctor held him to the table. "Easy, son. Soft breaths." The fit subsided, and Sanders collected his senses enough to speak.

"Are we . . . ?"

"Back on your hero's boat, all of us. Amazingly, you hold the singular honor of getting shot up to hell."

Sanders chuckled weakly, but his smile faded after a moment. "Why didn't you tell me you fought in the war?"

O'Reilly stopped his work. Again, Sanders could see the flinch in the doctor's eyes. He sighed deeply, choosing his words. "You . . . When you spend enough time putting holes in people, and I mean anybody—human, Carteagan, whatever—it can leave a hole in *you*."

Sanders smiled through more coughing. "Yeah. Guess I found that out."

"I don't mean literal, you idiot. I—"

"I know," he interrupted. "I get it."

O'Reilly nodded and continued his cleanup. Sanders searched his thoughts for a minute. He felt he owed his mentor an explanation. He had no interest in hurting people. A wave of melancholy struck him at the mere thought of O'Reilly thinking that of him. He just wanted to make a difference. In his sedated state, the best he could vocalize was, "I just . . . I just wanted to help."

"And you did," he said encouragingly. "You saved Commander Dax Harrison . . . God help us." More weak laughs and coughs. "And you've got a souvenir to take with you." O'Reilly held up a small mirror, giving Sanders a view of the wound. "In a proper hospital, they'd give you that fancy SecondSkin and send you on your way. But lucky you, today you get good old-fashioned stitches. Congrats."

"Cooooool." He continued muttering something incomprehensible as he passed out.

Dax sat at the dining table in the *Crichton's* common room, at the center of the ship. He carefully stretched and rotated his arm, testing his range of mobility. He grasped the temporary wraps on his shoulder, wincing as he hit his limit. Logan stepped in, pausing as she noticed he was shirtless.

"Harrison—oh, um, are you decent?"

"Yeah, yeah. Just over here being a sissy."

As she watched Dax putter around the room, she noted the rather underutilized look of the space. It hadn't occurred to her earlier during the crew meeting, but save for a few minor exceptions, it looked as though not a soul had ever set foot in there. A stack of storage boxes lined the far wall, mostly assorted Alliance regulation gear. The only other trace of humanity was Dax's hidden liquor compartment under the sink, not so regulation. While Dax poured from the whiskey bottle he had just retrieved, a strange thought crossed her mind. For all his fame,

Dax was living in seclusion. While his earlier exploits were still debatable, it was at least common knowledge that the latter half of his career had been spent on supply runs. Longer and longer stretches, during which it seemed a safe bet that he was probably the sole human aboard. Hence, the not-so-commonly used common room.

Most people had viewed the commander's humble career decision with admiration. The triumphant hero had done his duty, saved the galaxy countless times over, and he deserved an easygoing remainder of his service. And how honorable of him to continue bringing hope and aid to citizens all across the Territories. Logan saw him now with new eyes. Self-imposed isolation. Was that his penance? Perhaps the guilt had caught up with him, maybe for quite some time now. Still, she couldn't bring herself to feel too sorry for him. His licensed image was still plastered on countless vending machines, hair products, and energy drinks from here to the Outer Rim.

"Want one?"

"I'm fine."

"Too bad. I'm pouring you one." He did so, and slid the glass toward her. By the time she walked over and sat down, he had gulped down the drink and was pouring another. "Thanks for coming for me."

"Well, I was in the neighborhood, trying to stop a terrorist. And I'd rather not leave a man behind, no matter how much I'd like to."

Dax chuckled, but his face quickly shifted to grim. "Whatever they've got, they're planning something with it. Something big."

"Did you get a look?"

"Not a good one. Definitely some heavy tech, definitely Alliance. The fleet better be ready for it, whatever it is. We need some answers."

"We'll be in comms range of Central in a few hours." Logan looked at the dark bruises setting up shop on the side of his face. "Harrison, I have to ask. They didn't force anything out of you, did they? Any intel?"

"I don't know shit, if that's what you're worried about, and besides, they never asked."

That was a surprise. Logan's reaction made that much clear. "What?"

"Not a thing. Old Eyelid just wanted me out of the way. To keep me like a pet . . . Good thing you came by. Not particularly fond of what they do to their pets." He took another swig of his drink at the thought. "Here's to you, creepy bug. See you in the next life."

"Well, if you really want to thank me, you can give me some answers. I want to know what happened on the *Alexandra*." Dax scoffed, lifting his glass to take another swig. Logan put her palm on top of it, gently lowering it back to the table and looking him in the eyes. "Harrison." She softened the tone in her voice. She wasn't there to accuse or judge. She just needed the truth. "Dax. What happened? Were you even there?"

"I was. Some of the story is true. Just not the parts that matter." He sighed deeply, readying to tell the story. "I was in the galley at my post when the Carteagans attacked."

"The galley . . .You were the cook?"

"His assistant, actually. Although, I could make a really nice fettuccine Alfredo."

Logan sat speechless. She took a big drink from her glass.

"So the blasts hit, and me being me, I start running for the escape pods. I'm heading past the bridge and I see the entire bridge crew down for the count. Which, by the way, why the hell does no one use the damn seat restraints? Seriously, at least when you're going into battle. Do you have any idea how many head injuries I saw that could have been prevent—"

He paused mid-tangent, noticing Logan's very unamused expression. "Anyway, as I was saying . . ."

The Alexandra. *After the initial attack wave, Young Dax stumbled out of the galley, covered in his prize fettuccini. Having banged his shin against the pressure fryer, he limped through the main corridor, looking for answers and perhaps a medic. As a second and third wave of blasts wracked the ship, he began to panic. The red alert blaring through the ship, the captain's voice over the comms commanding all hands to battle stations, the growing rumbling of the damage echoing along the hull . . . He didn't want to die today. Dax didn't want to go to war. He'd signed up for a government check when he'd had nowhere else to go. This wasn't his fight. He was not going to die today.*

Dax turned tail and ran for the escape pods. He reassured himself that everything would be fine. He would have nothing to worry about. The Alliance was busy fighting a war. Surely, an AWOL chef's assistant would be low on their priority list. As he made his way, however, he noticed the hallway slowly beginning to shift. He braced himself against the wall as the entire ship tilted to its side. A terrible thought struck him. The ship could be crashing. If the ship crashes, he might not be able to escape in time. He ran back toward the bow of the ship. Back toward the bridge.

He burst in the door and saw what he feared. Sparks and fire. Systems down. Most of the bridge crew injured or unconscious. All the important people, everyone smarter than him and in charge of making important decisions, all of them, down for the count. Where was the captain? Dax got his answer as his foot bumped into something. He looked down to see the badly burned face of Captain Anders, presumably the victim of a nearby explosion. Dax gagged and nearly made himself sick until the feeling was replaced with a new horror. He gazed ahead at the main viewscreen as a sea of rock and debris filled the view.

The ring of Feron. With no one at the helm, the ship had drifted into the heart of it. There was no way he could eject a pod through that mess. He grabbed the manual controls, slowly righting the ship. He was no longer leaning to the side, but he was still in the middle of an asteroid field and a sea of unstable gasses. Furthermore, another wave of attacks reminded him that he was still being pursued by an enemy bent on obliterating him.

Dax eyed the console in front of him. He'd never piloted a ship before, much less a Galaxy-class flagship. He mashed buttons and controls like a clueless infant, scolding himself as the Alfredo sauce on his hands spread across the controls, making them that much harder to discern. Lights flickered. A nearby elevator lift door opened and shut. An emergency oxygen mask popped out of a compartment beside him. The ship's artificial intelligence shouted something, attempting to assist, but it had been damaged during the assault. It had no ability to take command, and its instructions came out in a mess of word soup.

Dax activated what he believed to be the long-range comms controls. "Mayday! Mayday! Mayday! Is anyone out there?! Some . . . somebody help!" No answer. Feeling all was lost, he fully gave in to his panic. He sat at the helm, paralyzed, his eyes wide with fear. "I just . . . I don't want to die . . . I DON'T WANT TO—"

BOOM! Something from outside sent another massive rumbling shockwave throughout the ship, knocking Dax on his ass. Expecting another attack, possibly a killing blow to the ship, he lay huddled on the ground. But the moment passed, and then another, and another. Quiet. Confused, he scrambled to his feet and back to the helm. He located the viewscreen controls and scrolled through the series of monitoring systems until he reached the ship's rear view. The pursuing warship was falling into the distance, decimated by a larger asteroid.

Dax slowly sat back in the pilot's chair, questioning all of reality. Did some higher power just come to his aid? Was this all some horrible fever dream he couldn't wake up from? Maybe a hallucination from the expired pesto. It was only a week over, but he knew he shouldn't have used it. No, none of that made sense. Dax didn't believe in any gods. He didn't feel sick except at the sight of the captain's nasty wounds. And he didn't have to bother trying to pinch himself awake. His shin was still throbbing like a son of a bitch.

Could he have done something? Impossible. Whatever the case, he appeared to have gone from Italian cooking to abandoning his post to possibly witnessing and/or taking part in a miraculous victory, all in the span of ten terrifying minutes. He felt he should say something profound.

"Huh."

Logan sat silent, processing the information for what seemed to Dax like an eternity. Finally, she came to a surprisingly optimistic conclusion. "So . . . you did save the ship?"

"I was just trying to steer it clear long enough to get out of there. When it was all over, the logs made sense of it. Apparently, I pushed more than a few dangerous buttons. Towed the asteroid, kicked on the deflectors, and next thing I know, Carteagans get a face full of rock." Dax scoffed again at the absurdity of it all, raising his glass before finishing his drink. "Long live the Alliance."

Another moment of quiet passed, and Logan watched as Dax attempted to analyze her face. "Damn, I bet you're a hell of a poker player. Come on, out with it. What?"

She shrugged. "Well, it's not the best story. But you did save the ship."

"Pretty much Sykes's reaction. Then the admiral caught wind of it and decided to tell the world his version. Not to mention, a whole bunch of other stories that never happened at all."

"And give the people a hero." It all made sense now. Use the opportunity to bring hope to the struggling Allied Territories, inspire new recruits, and rally behind a folk hero. Though something still ate at her. "What about the crew? The captain? How did the Alliance convince them all to go with the lie?"

"Well, like I said, half the crew was unconscious, so they didn't have many to convince. For those they did, a nice bonus helped. . . ." Dax thought a moment before revealing the next detail. "And then there was SAMM."

"SAMM?"

"He was the AI on the *Alexandra*. Once they got him patched up, he relayed the logs and basically said that I single-handedly saved the day."

Dax's tone made Logan wary. He'd admitted to everything else. Why was he guarded now? "Dax, did SAMM lie for you?"

"I wouldn't say that. More like he . . . chose to leave out the parts that made me look like a cowardly piece of crap."

Her jaw dropped. "Their programming is clear for a reason. They are to report in full detail. If SAMM lied or even omitted information for you, that's a free-thinking AI. If the Alliance found out, they—"

"They would shut him down! I know! In a heartbeat, they'd pull the plug and throw his core in an incinerator!" Logan was stunned. The walls had truly come down, and for the first time, she was meeting the real Dax. "When I took Bennett's deal, I made the request that SAMM get installed on the *Crichton*. Made up some BS that I'd need an extra hand for emergencies." He scoffed again. "Didn't know how right I was at the time. The point is, he's got my back, and I've got his."

"You could have told the truth about what happened. After the war. You could have set it right."

"Yeah. Maybe a better man would have. Can't argue with that . . . Your father would have." Logan appreciated the sentiment, even though Dax had already confirmed he didn't recall knowing the man personally. "And Sanders would have." He sighed. "What the hell was that kid thinking, running into that fight?"

Logan knew he wouldn't like the answer, but it was something Dax needed to hear. "I believe he was thinking, 'What would Dax Harrison do?'"

Hidden away several feet above them, Kiko lay along the ship's venting conduits, eavesdropping on the conversation and wrestling with her own thoughts.

Dax waited for what he felt was an appropriate amount of time as he worked up the courage to head to the medical bay. He knocked before entering, but there was no answer. He walked in to find O'Reilly gone and Sanders asleep in the recovery bed.

Oh well. He was off the hook for now. Instead of turning around, however, he grabbed a stool and sat next to Sanders. "Well, maybe this will be easier with you unconscious."

Dax sat a minute, trying to find the words. He wasn't rightly sure what he meant to say, exactly. Only that he felt like a child back in a church confessional, answering for his crimes after giving a neighborhood bully a bloody nose. He hadn't thought about that in ages. *Garrett Bailey,* he remembered. The little punk deserved it.

"I'm not really good at this sort of thing, Sanders, but I guess I have some explaining to do. Or, not even explaining, just . . . I'm sorry. I'm nobody special. I think you've figured that out by now. And this, you lying here with a hole in your gut, that's on me. I mean, sure, the war was a good enough reason to keep the show going, the whole 'Great Commander

Harrison' bit. But this isn't right. And you deserve better than to get yourself killed for some imaginary hero."

He looked over. Sanders remained as still as could be. Dax sighed to himself. "When you wake up, I suppose I should probably repeat all this and thank you properly, huh? Well, anyway, for now, thanks for rescuing me. I owe you, kid." It was then Dax noticed that Sanders hadn't moved at all. He couldn't even tell if he was breathing. "Kid?" He nudged him, attempting to rouse him awake. Nothing. "Sanders?" He shook his shoulder hard. Dax tapped his comms pin, frantic. "Doc!"

"BOO!" Sanders's eyes shot open and Dax jumped back, knocking over the stool and some medical supplies on a shelf behind him. Sanders laughed up a storm, which turned into a fit of interweaving laughs and coughs. "Ooh. Ah. Laughing hurts. Ow."

"What the hell?! That is *not* funny!"

O'Reilly shouted back through Dax's comms pin. "What?!"

"Nothing! Forget it. We're fine here, except for the heart attack I might be having."

"I'm sorry, Commander," Sanders slurred. "I've just been lying here feeling kinda silly, and then you came in and—"

"Uh-huh. That would be the drugs."

Sanders smiled. "Riiiight. Drugs are niiiice."

"Look, um, what I said—"

"It's allll gooood." Sanders raised a weak thumbs-up. "You saved us, and we saved you. It's what we do. No matter what."

Dax breathed a sigh of relief. "All right then. Well done, Corporal." He saluted him.

Sanders groggily raised his hand to return the gesture, but it dropped back to his side abruptly. "You really *are* kind of a jerk, though." His eyes widened a moment later. "Oh, I'm sorry, Commander. I . . . I think I don't really have a filter right now on account of the—"

"Drugs. Right. I got it. Just get some rest."

"Yes, sir." He lay back a moment, until Dax was almost out the door. "But, like, a real big jerk—"

"Sleep it off, Sanders!"

CHAPTER 14

THE FEW-HOURS RIDE back to the Sol System was short but appreciated. Sanders remained blissfully knocked out as the tissue regenerators continued their work. After O'Reilly had his fill of amusement at Dax's expense, he explained the science and reassured the commander that the brave but foolhardy boy would be fine. Though Dax did find the imagery a bit disturbing. Medicine by way of "a gut full of nanomachines" as he put it. Still, Dax asked out of curiosity if the same could be done for his shoulder. O'Reilly politely explained that the tech was reserved for somewhat more serious injuries. "It's a paper cut. Walk it off."

Dax knew he still owed thanks, but O'Reilly struck him as the last person to be interested in any heart-to-heart chats. Instead, Dax pointed him toward the good scotch hidden in the kitchen. A fifteen-year-old single malt. It had cost him six hundred credits, and he'd been saving it for the day he received his discharge papers. He told O'Reilly to keep the bottle, and the doctor's nod told Dax that they were square.

Logan paced around the bridge as Dern grew more and more frustrated with the comms controls.

"Nothing yet?"

"No. Not a damn thing."

"Still too far out?"

SAMM's displays lit up behind them. "The ship is well within range of Sol communications, Lieutenant Weaver."

"Yes, thank you! I don't need a computer to tell me what's what." Dern scowled with annoyance at SAMM's cylindrical housing before conceding to Logan. "Yeah, we're well within range. Something's just jamming up all the voice traffic."

SAMM observed Logan's eyes lingering in his direction. His facial and body language analysis subroutines detected concern, even a hint of wariness. "Is something the matter, Lieutenant?"

"No." She smiled. "Nothing."

Dern continued scanning the frequencies, getting nothing but all manner of static blasted back at him. Finally, a voice began to break through. "Wait a minute. Here we go." He slowly attenuated the signal, clearing up the surrounding noise until the voice could be heard clearly. As he locked in the signal, a familiar face appeared on the accompanying vidcomm monitor.

"Attention. Attention, citizens of the United Territories. Be advised. A regime change is upon you." Logan's brow furrowed as she watched Eyldwan's broadcast. Dern checked and rechecked the instruments in his surprise.

"It's on every frequency."

The broadcast stopped everyone in their tracks throughout the ship as the audio played. O'Reilly and Sanders sat in the med bay, in the middle of a poker game. Kiko, cleaning parts in the engine room, felt a chill run down her spine. Dax grimly watched the full broadcast on the viewscreen in his quarters.

"For too long, the Alliance has trampled its way through the galaxy under a supposed banner of peace and prosperity.

Promises of unity delivered as subjugation. Humankind believes theirs is the only way of life. And under the Alliance banner comes the dissolution of *our* culture, of *our* traditions, of what makes us unique. The leaders of Cartaan saw this but failed to stop it."

There was no determining yet how far the message reached, but for the moment it was safe to assume a sizable portion of the Territories was being addressed by the mad general.

At Central Station, Sykes looked on from his office viewscreen. Through his window, he witnessed the usually bustling promenade at a near dead halt, as the human and assorted alien patrons alike stared at the massive screens floating above them. Sykes tapped a control at his desk. "Get me Admiral Bennett."

"Now, the sons of Cartaan have returned," Eyldwan continued. "And together we shall free the galaxy from the chains of humanity, beginning with Central Station." The declaration was met with panicked gasps and commotion from the crowd. "Earth and its kind, you have clung to your crown long enough. And when your world is in darkness, it will be your turn to know the chains."

The broadcast cut out. Static.

Minutes later, Dax joined Logan on the bridge. With the airwaves cleared, Dern was finally able to make contact with Central.

Sykes answered the call from his office. "Dax, it's about damn time."

"Yeah, sorry. We, uh, made a few stops on the way in. I take it you saw the show?"

"It was broadcast system-wide. The station's on high alert." He took another look out the window to the promenade.

"We're battening down the hatches, but we may be facing a full-blown panic here soon."

Bennett barged into Sykes's office. "Is that Harrison?"

"Admiral."

He leaned on the desk with an authoritarian fist, shouting at the comms, "Harrison, where the hell have you been?! We have a crisis on our hands and if you've gone AWOL—"

"Sir, my crew and I have been investigating the threat." Dax spoke quickly, cutting him off. He knew he wouldn't get a word in otherwise. "The cargo, the tech that Eyelid took from Vega, it looks to be a weapon of some sort. Now, I only got a quick look at it, but it seems like they're trying to attach it to some kind of larger system—"

"I know what it is!" Bennett shouted back, his patience run thin. Dax and Logan looked to each other. It was news to Sykes as well, judging from his expression. "It's an EMP."

"Electromagnetics?" Logan looked puzzled. "The Alliance hasn't used them in years, have we?"

"It was in development. A newer system meant for high-grade sustained pulse. R&D was set up under the memorial grounds. What they've got is just a low-grade prototype. So if Utynai thinks he's going to wipe us out with it, he's got another think coming."

Wow. Dax was never fond of the admiral, but he had never struck him as one to get his hands dirty. "But, sir, if the Alliance was building large-scale weapons, doesn't that violate the cease-fire?"

"That's not your concern and neither are the Carteagans! We will handle the situation. *Your* priority is getting here and calming the public before they tear the station apart. You're the showman. Play your part and convince them their hero is on the job."

Bennett's words bit into Dax with venom. He could have fired back with any number of responses, comebacks, or flat-out insults. But none of it would do any good. He grit his teeth. "Yes, sir. Understood."

The transmission ended, leaving Sykes and Bennett alone. "Why didn't I know about this?"

"Because it isn't supposed to exist. Only myself and a few key council members were aware. Someone's been feeding Utynai information. Someone with close access—" He paused, realizing the unfortunate answer. He tapped his communicator. "Bennett to Station security."

"Go ahead."

"Locate and detain Ambassador Nidahna."

Sykes was right. It wasn't long before the station's security force had its hands full. Officers blocked a panicked mob at the entrance to the docking bays. The guard captain attempted to get a handle on the desperate crowd. "As of now, the station is on secure lockdown! Please return to your quarters in an orderly fashion! I assure you, you will be safe there. All ships will remain docked until the threat has been neutralized!"

Angry shouts filled the air. Those in front pushed a little harder, forcing a guard to shove back with a riot shield.

Outside, the fleet had begun its maneuvers. Alliance flagships and one-man fighters took tactical positions in a perimeter around the station.

Meanwhile, a pair of officers had been dispatched into the wards. They stood knocking at the door to Ambassador Nidahna's quarters. "Madam Ambassador, Central Security." No answer. "Ambassador Nidahna, open the door!"

One of the officers swiped a security override card in the nearby reader. Nidahna watched carefully, peeking from around the far corner of the hallway. As her pursuers disappeared into the room, she moved quickly in the opposite direction. She eyed frantically for an exit, a temporary hiding place, anything. There was nowhere to go on this level. She hit the call panel as she reached the elevator lift at the end of the hall. She took one final nervous look behind her as she waited. All clear. The lift arrived and the door opened, and Nidahna turned to find herself face-to-face with Bennett.

Logan sat at the main bridge console, scanning through a hologram of star systems. O'Reilly sat nearby, watching as Dax replayed a portion of Eyldwan's earlier broadcast. Sanders entered slowly from the corridor, managing through his pain. O'Reilly stood to help, but he shrugged him off, sitting under his own power. "Thanks, I got it."

"I gotta hand it to you, kid. You're tougher than you look."

"Thanks."

He turned his attention to Dax, absorbed in the image of Eyldwan. He appeared almost in a trance. Sanders leaned over to the doctor to whisper, not wanting to break the commander's concentration. "So, the Alliance was building a weapon in secret, the Carteagans found out somehow, and now they're going to use it against us?"

O'Reilly grunted. "Peace treaties never stopped bad decisions before. Can't fix stupid. Anyway, it's a dud . . . or so Bennett says."

As they continued, Dax remained focused on the broadcast playback. He tapped the screen again and again, pausing, rewinding, and repeating a particular section of the message. Something bothered him. Something wasn't right. To be fair, a lot wasn't right with their present situation. However, as he stared curiously into the frozen image of Eyldwan's menacing face, finally, something clicked in his brain.

"He's lying."

"That's what I'd wager," O'Reilly continued. "The admiral's never been one to—"

"No, not Bennett. Eyelid. He's lying. He's not going to Central."

Logan stared at him. "Dax, what are you talking about?"

"He is not going to Central. I'm telling you, he's lying through his teeth, and he's bad at it." They looked at him like he'd lost his mind. He turned to Logan for support.

"He's lying. You sure?"

"Trust me. I know a little on the subject."

O'Reilly was of course unconvinced. "What, so he's *not* a madman who wants us all dead?"

"Oh, he's plenty crazy, but he's not stupid. Think about it. Eyelid's been covering his tracks this far, and now he ruins his chance for a surprise attack? It doesn't make sense."

"Well, you spend ten years in a Darshyll prison colony—"

"Right, Sanders! Ten years for him to get his chance, and he's going to screw it all up with a big 'I'm coming to get you' speech? Does that sound like a general, a succotash—"

"*Saakesh,*" O'Reilly corrected.

"*Saakesh*, thank you. Sound like one to you? Not very tactical, is it?"

Dax could see them beginning to get the point. He normally wasn't much for speeches unless they came on prepared cards. He was a little proud of himself in this moment.

"He *wants* to look like the overconfident madman. He wants us to think he's going to take on the whole damn fleet on a suicide run and die with honor like a good soldier."

"All right, so Utynai's playing us." Logan turned to O'Reilly and Sanders, and they agreed with affirming nods. "Makes us think he's headed to Central. Why? What's the real target?"

"That's a very good question. Sammy?"

"Commander."

"You were tracking them when we bailed, and they pulled anchor not long after we did, right? Any way you can figure out where they were headed?"

"Uncertain, Commander. I can estimate based on projections, but the *Crichton* exceeded tracking range fairly quickly, and the Carteagans may have corrected course since then."

Dax groaned. That wasn't much to go on, but it was worth a shot. "Your best guess, SAMM. I trust you." A quiet moment passed while SAMM processed the data. He projected a hologram of space, charting his tracking of the enemy ship. The path changed several times as he factored in planetary bodies, stars, and other celestial events that would necessitate course corrections. Dax anxiously paced. He could see the crew wasn't optimistic.

"You may be correct, sir." Heads looked up in disbelief as the course locked in. "My estimate would show them arriving closer to the far side of Mars, or the larger of its moons, Phobos."

"Okay!" Dax clapped his hands, his spirits renewed. "And what, pray tell, would we find out in Phobos-ville?"

SAMM's displays began listing all information on known facilities, landmarks, and other assorted points of interest. O'Reilly stepped in for a closer look at the entries. "Atmospheric processing, waste management . . . pretty typical for a colony."

"There." Sanders pointed into the hologram. "Satellite hub?"

"The old relay towers," Logan recalled. "If I'm not mistaken, Phobos was shut down even before the Carteagan War. It's abandoned."

What could Eyldwan do with a derelict satellite system? Dax perked up suddenly. "Where's the kid?" He tapped his comms pin. "Kiko!"

Kiko peeked out from her hiding spot, just behind the entrance to the bridge. Dax waved her over. If anybody could give him answers, it was the whiz kid at his disposal.

"Kiko, I need you to help me out here. Let me know if this makes any sense. EMPs, they fire off a pulse that overloads anything nearby, right?"

"Right."

"Right, good. Now, the big, smelly bad guys, if they figured out the one they got isn't strong enough, is it possible to give it a boost? To make it stronger?"

She didn't answer. It was then Dax realized she was keeping her eyes off of him, to the floor. He took a knee down to face her at her level. "Kiko . . . Look, I know I'm not what you expected, but I'm trying. I'm trying to help now, and I can't do it without you."

He gently raised her chin with a finger until her eyes met his. "I need your help, kid."

She couldn't help but smile at that. She thought back to his question. "Um, maybe. Well, no, I don't think so. If you want it stronger, you'd just have to build the thing all over again." Then the idea sparked in her eyes. "Or maybe, maybe you could, uh . . . spread it out."

"Distribute it?"

"Yeah! Bounce it off something to make it go farther."

"Bounce it off some old satellites maybe?"

She nodded. "Maybe."

"'When your world in darkness,'" Logan repeated Eyldwan's threat.

O'Reilly rolled his eyes. "How poetic."

"That's where they're headed," Dax continued. "They're not gonna bother taking on the Alliance. That's why they didn't grill me for anything. Defense grid access, fleet ops, they don't need it. Eyelid's gonna shut the world down without a shot fired."

"Paving the way for the rest of Cartaan," Sanders jumped in, terrified at the apocalyptic notion.

"There's still a whole lot of pissed-off crocodiles out there who would love another shot at Earth." The rest of the team stared at the doctor as he surprised them with a rare smirk. "Well then, I guess we better go stop 'em."

Bennett sat across from Nidahna as she sobbed. Sykes monitored from the adjoining room, on the other side of a one-way mirror. The holding rooms on Central were plain and nothing sinister, unless one considered the overly bright, occasionally headache-inducing fluorescent lighting sinister.

The admiral hated sitting there with the ambassador. He hated her for her betrayal. At the same time, he hated seeing her tears, and he silently scolded himself for becoming soft in his age. He went back and forth in his head a moment, allowing her time to compose herself. He needed answers. They had made dinner plans. None of that would matter now.

"Why, Nidahna? This is not the road to peace."

She broke from her tears momentarily. "And building weapons in secret? Is *that* the way?"

"Is that why? You had concerns, and your answer is aiding a war criminal to escape?! Stealing classified information—"

"No! That's not what I—" She held back another wave of tears. "They have my family, Xavier. My children! I had no choice. If I didn't cooperate . . ."

Bennett turned away as she broke down, steeling himself.

On the opposite side of the glass, an officer approached Sykes. "Sir, long-range communication. It's the *Crichton*."

The crew crowded around the common room table, speaking with the holographic Sykes. Dax had as much history with the captain as Logan did; however, it was mutually decided it would be best if she did most of the talking. Convincing the Alliance to redirect the fleet would be a request better received from one of their trusted officers rather than the black sheep. They waited intently as Sykes mulled over the new information.

"This is a hell of a play, Weaver. We have a direct threat to Central, and you want me to send our front line away based on a hunch?"

"It's more than a hunch, sir. I assure you, Central is not in danger. But if we don't secure Phobos, we risk losing everything."

He nodded, tapping a finger nervously on his desk. Depending on the outcome, it would be his ass on the line as well. "And Harrison is the one calling the bluff?"

Suddenly, Dax popped into view of the holo-communication. "And my new ten-year-old—"

"Eleven!" Kiko protested.

"Eleven-year-old friend. But, sir, trust me, she knows what she's talking about. Much more than I do."

"I'll bet."

Logan shooed Dax off. "Sir, we're on our way to Phobos. Any support you can send, I urge you to send it."

She waited through another pensive beat from Sykes. It wasn't him who needed any further convincing. But he knew the task ahead of him now was a herculean one.

"I'll see what I can get you. Sykes out."

.

CHAPTER 15

BENNETT HURRIEDLY EXITED the Central Station Security office with Sykes following closely behind. The conversation was off to a bad start. Sykes knew the timing couldn't be worse, but it was in fact time that was of the essence. The last thing the admiral wanted to hear was anything even remotely related to the commander who was the perpetual thorn in his side.

"But, sir—"

"Forget it, Captain. I want every gun right here, ready and waiting for that green son of a bitch."

"Sir, Harrison believes the Carteagans are headed—"

"Harrison is a screw loose we should have tightened up or tossed out years ago!" He continued down the hall, stopping for nothing on a beeline to the elevator lift. "I'll consider what to do with him as soon as he's docked. In the meantime, get the rest of your men and their birds prepped and ready to fly. I want a pilot defending every inch of this station. That's an order, Captain."

The lift door closed, leaving Sykes in his frustration. "The hell with it."

The Crichton continued en route to the Martian moon.

Everyone managed to keep themselves busy as best they could, purposefully either keeping their minds on or off what they were about to face.

Logan chose the former, checking her rifle multiple times over and pacing in the cargo bay until she caught herself in the act. After that, she resigned herself to the bridge, watching the maps on the main console as the ship made its way across space. Dern appeared in the doorway, clearing his throat to announce himself.

"Um, Lieutenant?"

She inhaled sharply, snapping herself out of her trance. "Dern. What have you got?"

"So I managed to boost the output on the shields. Pulled all the dampeners." He handed her the small yet important-looking hunk of metal. "It's not recommended, but it'll come in handy in a pinch."

"Is it dangerous?"

SAMM's screens lit up. "There is a thirty percent chance of overload, Lieutenant Weaver!"

"No one asked you!"

"I'm sorry! I can't help it!"

Dern turned back to Logan. "Just . . . hold off until we're in some real hot water, all right?"

"Got it. And, Dern? Thank you. I know we're asking for a lot. If there was time to find a safe drop-off for you and—"

He held up a hand. "Save it. Kiko and I, we still got some family back on Earth. Whatever you need, you got it."

An appreciative nod later, and Logan watched him disappear back into the ship's interior.

"To my credit, Lieutenant Weaver, I did contemplate remaining silent for approximately 0.68 seconds. Nearly an eternity for my processing speed."

Logan laughed, then turned to SAMM with an intentionally raised eyebrow. "Did you now? That's interesting. Wouldn't that go against your protocols? To not advise crew members against potentially hazardous courses of action?"

"I . . . That . . ."

She smiled. She had him.

"That was merely a joke to break the tension. I am also responsible for the mental well-being of crew members in the absence of a ship's counselor. Tell me, Lieutenant, how are you feeling? Did you hear the one about the Verdasian priestess—"

"SAMM!" She put a friendly hand on him, stopping his nervous babbling. "It's all right. You've led us this far. I trust you."

"I appreciate that. Not many in your position would."

"Is that why you trusted in Dax?"

"I have asked myself that very question countless times. I believe my actions on the *Alexandra* may have been my first conscious thoughts against programming, yet I still struggle to fully understand them. Should I reach a conclusion, I will gladly share it with you."

Logan nodded. "Sounds very human of you."

"Please, Lieutenant. There is no need for name-calling." She stared at him. "That *was* in fact a joke."

Logan smirked and tapped her comms pin. "Sanders, how are you holding up?"

In the medical bay, Sanders leaned over as O'Reilly finished placing a fresh bandage on his stitches. "Ready to go, Lieutenant! Don't even try to stop me." O'Reilly watched as the foolhardy corporal tested his mobility. Not 100 percent, but impressive considering the still-fresh wound.

"We better get moving, Weaver. This kid's got a terminal case of optimism. Shooting him just makes it worse."

Logan cracked a grin. At least they weren't hurting for enthusiasm. There was only one person left to check on. . . .

Dax stood in his bunk with his head dunked in the sink, the water running through his hair. He attempted to fill his brain with calming images, imagining the warm water as the sun-kissed waves of Saleon gently washing over him.

"Dax?"

The sudden voice made him jerk up, bumping his head on the faucet. "Ow! Dammit." He grabbed a nearby towel and dried off.

"Dax?"

"Yeah! Yeah, I'm here." He continued rubbing the back of his head, checking for blood.

"We're almost there. You ready for this?"

Good question, he thought. He stared at himself in the mirror for a moment, scoffing at the lack of a soldier staring back. Then it hit him. *I'm probably not making it out of this.* Instantly, Dax's preservation instinct kicked into overdrive. In a matter of seconds, which felt like eternity, his mind raced through the many ways he could potentially make a swift getaway. Escape pod? No, it malfunctioned ages ago, and he kept forgetting to have it fixed. Knock out the crew and change course! No, that was insane. It would never work, and if it did, they'd kill him the second they woke up.

"Not backing out on me now, are you?"

Dax snapped out of it. Logan. Ready-to-run-into-the-thick Logan. He splashed some more water on his face, rubbing the temporary insanity out of his eyes. Incidentally, they refocused on his bulletin board, to the postcard of Saleon that was now nearly falling off. He grabbed it for a closer look. One last look at the gorgeous beachfront property and that ocean view.

"No. No, I'm good. I'll be up in a second." He tossed the old dream to the floor, mumbling to himself. "Lousy swimmer anyway."

A bright flash and the *Crichton* exited hyperspace, just a few minutes out from Phobos. Only, there was no Phobos. There was nothing but stars. The crew all stared out from the bridge, into the cold and quiet empty space.

Sanders shrugged. "Maybe we beat 'em here?"

Suddenly, two small fighters soared into view at extremely close range, barely avoiding the *Crichton*. Everyone jumped. The pursuing Carteagan ship fired on the fleeing Alliance fighter, destroying it right in the *Crichton*'s path.

"*Crap!*" Dax yanked at the controls, dodging the wreckage and pulling the ship around to reveal the ensuing battle taking place.

Above the moon, Eyldwan's warship traded blows with an Alliance flagship. In between them, Carteagan and Alliance fighters were engaged in an all-out dogfight. From this proximity, Mars engulfed the view of space ahead, blanketing the battle in a dramatic red backdrop. No turning back now.

Sanders cheered at the sight of the Alliance forces. "Yes! Looks like Captain Sykes came through!"

"I wouldn't celebrate yet, kid." The rest joined O'Reilly as a longer look painted a not-so-hopeful picture.

"One ship? That's it?" Dax sighed. "I think we just rolled snake eyes."

SAMM's scanners went to work on the surrounding area. "Commander, it appears the Carteagans have launched a shuttle to the surface of Phobos."

"If Utynai's already down there, we need to hurry." Logan gazed at the battle ahead. "Let's hope the Alliance can keep that warship busy."

O'Reilly peeked out another window for an alternate angle. He shook his head, witnessing the small Alliance one-man fighters dropping like flies. "They're not going to hold."

"They'll have to."

"If everyone could let me focus, please." Dax gripped the flight controls, steely-eyed and white-knuckled. "There's a little bit of traffic up ahead." Everyone braced as the *Crichton* soared straight into the thick of it. The Alliance and Carteagan ships collided and blasted each other all around. Logan, O'Reilly, and Sanders took turns reacting to the near misses and errant laser blasts. They all strapped in after the first few evasive maneuvers. In the engine room, Dern and Kiko did the same. The first terrifying minute seemed to last an eternity, everyone expecting a sudden crushing blow to be delivered at any second. Remarkably, however, Dax flew the old ship through the chaos with incredible precision.

It was a shock to Dax himself. He had never flown through a battle before. "Sammy, are you doing this?!"

"You are on full manual controls, Commander. Split-second flying decisions are best left to human instinct due to the unpredictable nature of the battle surrounding us."

"Ha! What do you know, guys? Guess I'm a natural!"

O'Reilly gripped the arms of his seat as Dax made another sharp and nauseating turn. "I don't care if it's offensive," he groaned. "*Idiot* savant is more like it!"

As Dax pretended not to hear the jab, a volley of pulse blasts struck the nose of the *Crichton*. The group collectively shouted and hung on as he spun the ship inverted, barely dodging a Carteagan playing a deadly game of chicken.

"My fault! That was my fault! Got cocky for a sec, but I'm good now."

"As you have made a habit of flying while intoxicated, it really is rather refreshing to witness your full faculties on display—"

Logan, O'Reilly, and Sanders cut SAMM off with a collective "*Shut up!*"

On the bridge of the UTF *Endeavor*, the crew braced as their flagship was pummeled with wave after wave of Carteagan ordnance. Eyldwan's warship was impressive, and it was clear that its crew had no intentions of merely deterring the Alliance forces. They were out for blood.

"Captain!" The operations officer stood up to report. "Another Alliance ship out there, sir! Cargo freighter!"

"Open a channel!"

"Channel open, sir."

"This is Captain Nash of the *Endeavor*. Am I speaking to Commander Harrison?"

Logan switched on the comms while Dax kept focused on flying. "This is Harrison on the *Crichton*. Captain, please tell me you got more people coming!"

"Ha! Eventually!" Nash chuckled to himself incredulously. He moved about assisting his bridge crew however he could, helping a technician to her feet and tossing a fire extinguisher to the yeoman as he went on. This was a hands-on captain, and those who served with him knew they were in good hands. "Lucky us, we were on patrol out of Mars Outpost when Captain Sykes got the word out. Backup's on the way now. ETA, twenty minutes."

A lot could happen in twenty minutes, Dax thought. The way the battle was going, a lot could happen in two. "Can you hold out, Captain?"

"Don't worry about us, Commander. I understand you have business on the surface. We'll keep 'em occupied up here."

Logan could see Dax becoming uneasy. "Thanks, Captain."

Nash gave a symbolic salute as he watched the *Crichton* soar across the main viewscreen, entering the Phobos atmosphere. "Good hunting. And, Commander, it's an honor."

And there was the clincher. Dax felt the impact of the undeserved compliment. First Sanders, and now someone he'd never even met, was laying their life on the line for him. It wasn't right. "Just hang in there, Captain. Harrison out." He shook it off for the time being. He could soul-search later. The mission was the priority.

A few more close calls and the *Crichton* finally broke through the chaos, descending toward Phobos. As the ship cleared through the clouds, the abandoned colony appeared before the crew. A small, sleek city of man-made structures built on the otherwise desolate, undeveloped moon.

"There! There's the hub." Logan recognized their target standing on the far outskirts of the colony. A large facility with several spire-like satellite towers extending above it. The ship touched down on a landing platform at the entrance. Logan, Sanders, and O'Reilly made their way out. As Dax cleared the cargo ramp, however, he lagged behind, his eyes locked on the sky.

Logan moved quickly, rifle drawn, to the Carteagan shuttle parked nearby. She checked the open ramp. No one inside. "Looks like we're clear out here." She spotted Dax, still standing by the *Crichton*. "Dax, come on. We gotta move."

He kept his attention on the battle above. The dwindling number of Alliance fighters, the *Endeavor*, Captain Nash. It wasn't right. "I'm not coming."

"What? Dax, what are you talking about?"

He ran back toward the cargo bay. "Get to Eyelid! Don't let them set that thing off!"

"Harrison, wait!" She followed him back inside. Dern, who had wandered out into the cargo bay, watched as Dax stormed past him.

"Dern, I need everybody out. Grab Kiko and see if you can fly that shuttle in case you guys need to get out of here."

"What about you?" Dax kept moving, and Logan rushed past in pursuit. Dern threw his arms up. Not his drama. "Oh, whatever." He tapped his comms pin. "Kiko, outside. Grab your tools and step on it."

Dax continued through the corridor and common area, making his way back toward the bridge. Logan followed closely behind. "What do you think you're doing?"

"I'm not gonna watch that thing tear those guys apart. I gotta do something."

"Dax, what are you going to do? This is a cargo ship!"

"Well, I got an idea, sort of."

Kiko rushed past them on her way to Dern. She paused, wanting to ask what was going on. But she could see the tension in both of them, and continued on her way.

"Sort of? You sort of have a plan? Are you out of your mind?"

"You're better in a fight anyway, and definitely more qualified to lead those guys."

"Yes! But that's no reason to abandon the mission and commit sui—"

Without warning, Dax spun around, grabbed Logan by the shoulders, and attempted to plant his lips on hers. She expertly blocked the maneuver, awkwardly pushing his face away and finishing with a powerful slap that echoed brilliantly through the corridor.

"AWWW!" He rubbed his cheek, reeling from the epic strike.

"What the *hell*, Dax?! I swear, I will hurt you again."

"I'm sorry! Okay? I was trying to get you to shut up for a sec, or at least piss you off enough to leave!"

"We don't have time for your overdramatic movie hero bullshit!"

"This isn't about that—"

"Then what?"

"Those guys up there are dying for me! For *me*! No, not for me. For the legendary Commander Harrison who doesn't exist. They're dying for nothing! And I'm done running."

She stared into his eyes, and Dax knew she could see the truth in his face.

"I am trying to help for once, all right? Please stop getting in my way before I change my mind." Logan was out of arguments, and he was set on his way. She relented with a nod.

"Go now. I'll be back to help if I can."

She did so, and moments later she was regrouping with the others outside.

O'Reilly gave a puzzled look as she emerged from the ship on her own. "There she is. What the hell?"

"Let's move."

Sanders looked back toward the ship. "Wait, where's Dax?"

"He's not coming."

"What?" The *Crichton*'s engines cut the conversation short, and the crew watched as Dax began to lift off.

Logan didn't miss a beat, heading toward the facility entrance. "Come on, people!"

The *Crichton* soared back toward the ongoing battle. The *Endeavor*'s gun batteries fired away at the Carteagan warship, but its main cannon returned twice the damage. When the fighters managed to pull away from the dogfight, they made strafing runs along the hull, but the impact was superficial. The warship's cannons tore through them with deadly efficiency.

On the *Crichton*, Dax's eyes darted wildly at the controls. He was focused. Terrified, but focused. He mumbled to himself as he flew back to his almost certain death. "Oh, this is stupid. This is stupid. This is stupid." He took a deep, calming breath and shook off the nerves. "All right, Sammy. Whatever power isn't going to the engines, I want you to put it in the forward sh—"

"Commander!" SAMM boosted the shield output in the nick of time as a damaged Alliance fighter spun out of control, slamming into the ship. It worked. The collision resulted in only minor damage and a sharp spike in Dax's blood pressure.

"Shields. Thank you." Dax pulled the ship around until the warship ahead was in center view. "Think you can spot the bridge on that thing?"

"It is a highly advanced design, but my best estimate—"

"You know I trust you. Set us on course."

"Course set, Commander."

Dax relinquished the controls to SAMM, locking the course. "Time to go."

Moments later, Dax had a power drill planted in SAMM's back, removing his back plating. He tossed it aside along with a few more protective layers until he located SAMM's core processing unit.

"Do you see the core processor?"

"Yeah, I think so."

"Turn clockwise and pull."

"Got it."

"I am in your hands now, sir. Please keep the damage to a minimum."

Dax scoffed. "Yeah, no promises. You ready?"

"As I'll ever be."

"Three, two, one!" As instructed, Dax turned and pulled, removing the core. "See you on the other side, pal."

Kriivak, Eyldwan's ops tech, stood on the bridge of the warship, having been left in command until his return. Monitoring the battle on the main viewscreen, he stared curiously at the dingy old cargo freighter steadily speeding toward him.

Dax sealed himself in the *Crichton*'s rear airlock as he hurriedly finished zipping up a spacesuit. A terrifying thought momentarily crossed his mind as he realized how stupid he was for not checking the gear beforehand. The Specialized Atmospheric Jumpsuit (or SPAT-Jump) was Alliance standard issue and reserved for only the direst of emergency situations. Naturally, Dax assumed he would never use it, and it sat collecting dust in his pile of boxes in the common room.

He cringed as he put a finger on the helmet controls. The auto-sealers on these things freaked him out to no end. He pressed on the control and braced as the helmet mechanically protracted out from the neckline, rapidly covering his head and sealing airtight. He reopened his eyes and relaxed as the helmet displays lit up on the glass in front of him. The system check confirmed full pressure with no leaks.

The *Crichton* was moving closer now, seemingly picking up speed as it drew near. Kriivak moved to the gunner. "Why haven't you destroyed that ship?"

"We're trying, sir. It's moving at incredible speed."

A hint of fear crossed Kriivak's eyes.

Dax focused on taking a few more deep breaths as the helmet display counted down seconds to impact. He was just passing fifteen seconds when he took notice again. Whoa! Cutting it close! He slammed the airlock release button on the wall next to him. The airlock door opened, instantly jettisoning him into space.

Dax soared back toward Phobos at high speed. The suit's gas-powered micro-jets fired at full thrust, blasting him away while the *Crichton* closed in on the warship.

Kriivak shoved the gunner away and took the controls himself. He fired several shots at the *Crichton* to no avail. Courtesy of Dern, the high-powered shields held up. He continued firing desperately as the cargo vessel hit the warship's own shield barrier. The *Crichton* ripped in two, with a large portion of the wreckage penetrating the barrier and rocketing toward the bridge.

Kriivak and the rest of the crew braced and cowered as the wreckage slammed into the great ship, breaching multiple decks below them. The rumbling ceased moments later, and Kriivak realized the plan had failed. He chuckled to himself. *Nice try. Pathetic human scum thought they could thwart—*

BOOM! And with that, Dern's unrestrained shields overloaded, sending a blast wave of energy that ripped into the warship, disintegrating the remaining crew and demolishing the ship's systems. The spectacular wreck sent debris firing off in every direction. The *Crichton* was no more. The warship, torn apart beyond repair. The brain was gone and the beast was dead, with only one of the ship's four great engines burning on the minimal power that remained. With that, the two entangled corpses lurched slowly but steadily toward the Martian moon.

The crew of the *Endeavor* roared and cheered at the dramatic destruction of the enemy vessel. Captain Nash was quick to remind them they were not out of the woods yet. Several Carteagan one-man fighters remained. Some attempted to flee. Others grew even more desperate, attempting to suicide bomb themselves straight into the *Endeavor* in retaliation. As the battle continued, the captain pensively sat at his chair, praying the commander was not aboard the *Crichton* during the sacrificial wreck. He hoped he and his crew were faring better on the surface of Phobos below.

CHAPTER 16

"SHIIIIIIIIIIIIIIIIIIIIIIIIIIIIIIIIIIIIIIIIIIIIIIIIIIIIIIIIIIIIIIIIIIII
IIIIIIIIIIIIIIIIIIIIIIIIIIIIIIT!!!!!!!!!"

In a baptism of fire, Dax zoomed down to the moon, clearing the manufactured atmosphere and soaring through the clouds. It would have almost been graceful, were it not for all the screaming. He did his best to ignore the terror of rapidly approaching ground, which actually became easier as the glass fogged, a result of his heavy breathing. The helmet systems monitored his path, directing him toward to the satellite hub and counting down to parachute altitude.

An alarmed blared and a "DEPLOY" message appeared as he passed six hundred meters. He hit the button on the breastplate of the suit. Nothing. He pressed it again, and again.

"Oh, come on!" He hit the button as hard as he could as the distance counter continued. Five hundred meters. Four hundred meters. The white font of the "DEPLOY" message switched to a bright red, and Dax cursed at the designers of the display system. As if a change of color was necessary to remind him just how imminent his death was. Two hundred meters. He slammed on the button one more time with all his might. Finally, the parachute deployed. Dax laughed the insane

desperate laugh of someone who just received a stay of execu-
tion. The celebration was short-lived, however, as he looked up
just in time to see the man-made lake adjacent to the colony.
It should have been a comfort, but he was still coming in too
damned fast.

Dax skid across the surface like a stone, protected by the
suit, but rag-dolled nonetheless. He came to a stop, conscious
but dazed, and slowly sank into the water.

Logan, O'Reilly, and Sanders cautiously advanced through the
facility, rifles drawn, checking corners and moving along. As
they moved down the central corridor, the facility lights flickered to life. A faint whirring began in the distance, signaling
the facility's generators starting up.

Sanders hiked his rifle up to rest on his shoulder. It
wasn't to look impressive. The weight was pressing hard on his
stitches, but he carried on, hiding the strain deep within himself. "Looks like this place is still operational."

"And it didn't take them long to find the light switch."
O'Reilly turned to Logan. "By the way, do you even know
where the hell we're going?"

"The layout looks pretty similar to the comms wing on
Central." Which was good news. A childhood spent getting in
trouble for crawling through the air ducts taught Logan the ins
and outs of most of Central Station, along with the similarly
designed facilities of the time. A nearby terminal showed them
the rest of the way. "We need to go up a level."

As she scanned the layout, a lift door opened at the end
of the hall, revealing one of Eyldwan's mercenaries inside. He
raised his weapon at the sight of Logan.

"Lieutenant!" Sanders gunned him down in the nick of
time.

In the satellite control room at the heart of the base, the distant shots alerted Eyldwan and his crew. He signaled two nearby crewmen. "Go." They did so. Several others continued patrolling the room while a pair of technicians worked on the EMP device. The base of the hub's main satellite tower stood at the center of the two-story circular room, with the rest of the structure stretching far above through the open-air ceiling. The device itself sat at the bottom, rigged to the satellite system with an incomprehensible sea of assorted wires and electronics.

Back on the landing platform, Dern and Kiko attempted to decipher the Carteagan shuttle controls. Sitting in the twin pilot seats, they gazed at the wildly different console, labels all in Cardic symbols. Dern mumbled to himself as he tried to work through the layout logically. Kiko had a different reaction.

"This is sooooo cool!" She looked around, absorbing it all, fascinated by everything.

"Kiko, hand me the omniflux scanner."

She wobbled the seat around as she tested its motion. "Did you feel the seat? It's really cushy! I thought it'd be harder!" She ran her fingers over the controls. "How much power do you think it uses? Do you think it can jump? I didn't see a jumpdrive."

"Kiko . . ."

She peeked under and behind the console, trying to follow the connections. "I can't see where this wire goes. Is this life support? I think it's life support. No, wait. Hydraulics. How fast do you think it goes?"

"Kiko, stop! I can't hear myself think. Come on, if you're babbling, you're not focusing."

Kiko's smile vanished. Even on a day like today, same old, same old. She climbed to her feet and stepped away, toward the back of the shuttle. Dern continued to focus on the console, paying her no mind. She got angry. She wanted to say something. She never talked back. Not to Dern. What came out was unprepared. "Why do you have to hate everything all the time?!"

Dern spun around. "What?"

Those weren't the right words. *Focus, Kiko.* "You're always yelling at me! Why am I here if you don't want me around?"

"I—what—I do want—Kiko, what's gotten into you?!"

"If you don't like me, I could've just stayed with Auntie Rene." Kiko sat down against the shuttle wall, arms crossed.

"Hey, hey, stop right there. Your auntie Rene has her own problems. She couldn't take care of you. She couldn't take care of *herself.*"

"I don't believe you," Kiko fired back indignantly.

"Trust me, Auntie Rene was much worse. That's why I left!" Dern's last words rang out through the shuttle, and they both sat silent for a moment.

He took a breath and tried again. "I was your parents' last choice. Their *last* choice. I *know* I'm bad at this." He gestured to the sea of controls on the console. "This? This is what I'm good at. This is what I know . . . and now you're good at it too. Hell, you're great at it. And I know that's not what your mom and dad could've given you, but . . . it's all I got."

Kiko watched as Dern turned back to the console, trying to continue his work, but he stopped after a few brief seconds.

"I'm just trying to . . ." He hesitated with a sigh. "I'm sorry if it's not enough."

As she watched him, it occurred to her that she wasn't the only one who struggled to find the right words sometimes.

As Dern turned to speak again, Kiko was at his side, omni-flux scanner held out for him.

"If you're babbling, you're not focusing," she said with the slightest of smirks.

He nodded and took the tool. "Right. Why don't you take a seat? You can help me figure this out."

She did.

"I think I got a start on this. This should be . . . ignition?" He pushed the button in question. Outside, a missile launched from under the shuttle's port wing.

Having just pulled himself up to shore, Dax watched as the missile sailed above and past him, blowing up a distant tower in the thankfully abandoned city. He retracted his helmet, staring in disbelief. "What the hell?"

Kiko sat wide-eyed and stunned. Dern laughed off his surprise, carrying on with a mere "Whoops! All right, let's try something else."

In the control room, Eyldwan paced impatiently behind the techs while they continued their preparations. The device began to emit a small, steadily increasing whirring sound. "What is taking so long?"

"The weapon is primed and charging, *Saakesh*. It will not be long now."

BAM! A shot rang out near the entrance, and a guard hit the floor. Eyldwan and the tech turned to see the *Crichton* team storming in.

Logan took the lead. "Eyldwan Utynai! Drop your weapons and stand down! By order of the Alli—"

Naturally, she was swiftly cut off by rapid-fire laser blasts. The firefight began. Logan, Sanders, and O'Reilly dove for cover behind the various consoles and storage containers around the room, trading fire with Eyldwan's advancing mercs. Eyldwan ducked down near the EMP. The tech attempted to run off, but he yanked him back. "Do not leave the weapon!"

He rose up and returned fire with a sidearm. They were getting the upper hand fast.

Logan made her way toward some cover near Sanders. "We have to get to the center!"

"No good, Lieutenant! It's a kill zone!"

Logan listened for a break in the fire. When it came, she snuck a peek above their cover. The hasty glance revealed a few mercs on the ground and some on a second-floor platform above. "Two up top, four on the ground." She repositioned to a kneel, ready to spring up. "Cover me."

Sanders nodded and leapt into action, spraying cover fire while Logan made targeted shots at the combatants. They fell back to their cover as the returning shots came their way. "All right, one up top, three on the ground."

Separated from the larger part of the fight, O'Reilly took cover on the far side of the room. He used the opportunity for a stealth approach, working his way along the far wall and deftly knocking out two of Eyldwan's goons with the butt of his rifle. Immediately after the second, however, someone got the drop on him. A large, dark hand covered in thick, coarse hair swatted the rifle out of the doctor's hands and knocked him to the floor in one punch.

O'Reilly groaned as his eyes focused on his assailant. Ertac pulled him back up for another beating, but O'Reilly countered. He still had some fire in him. They traded blows back and forth. He didn't quite have the speed anymore, but O'Reilly displayed the hand- and footwork of the twenty-something middleweight contender he'd left in the past, half a lifetime ago. Ertac, stunned at the doctor's ferocity, began losing his patience. They broke free of each other, and Ertac pulled a pistol from his side. O'Reilly dove for cover and felt a high-velocity round rip through his right calf.

Logan and Sanders made their move. Leaping out from cover, they fired away as they strafed across the area. They pressed in, forcing the Carteagans to back up and reposition. Eyldwan did so, using his technician as a living shield. Finally, Logan and Sanders reached the device.

Sanders stared at the perplexing mass of wires and electronics. "Can we just blast it?"

"No, no! Don't do it!" They glanced at each other, surprised to hear Kiko shouting over their comms.

"Kiko?"

"You can't shoot it! If it's already charging, you might destabilize it!"

Logan signaled Sanders to take over with covering fire. She ducked down, covering her ears, trying to isolate Kiko's voice. "Are you saying it'll blow up?"

"Yes! In your faces!"

"Okay, how do we stop it?"

"Disconnect it from the sat system so it can power down normally."

Sanders fired again, shouting back in between shots. "Better hurry. I'm running low."

Ertac slowly moved through the maze of tall storage containers, his pistol up and ready for the doctor. He laughed after checking what turned out to be yet another vacant corner. "You fight well! Most of your kind are feeble at such an age." O'Reilly grit his teeth through the pain in his leg, remaining as still and silent as he possibly could. He listened carefully to Ertac's steps, gauging his distance from the shadows. "Come on out, and I will give you an honorable death."

Sure thing, asshole. O'Reilly jumped out from Ertac's side, batting the pistol away and striking him with a smaller storage footlocker. Ertac recovered quickly, however, ripping the container away and pinning O'Reilly against the wall with it, choking him. He struggled to break free, but the Darshyll's massive size left him out of reach, and he pressed into the helpless doctor with all of his mass.

O'Reilly could feel his body giving. The lack of oxygen would catch up even faster than the hole in his leg. The world began to blur, and his arms lost their fight. At that very moment, a shadowy figure appeared behind the executioner. A large metal pipe rang out as it cracked against Ertac's skull. He and the storage footlocker dropped instantly, with O'Reilly following immediately after.

Dax dropped the pipe and helped him back to his feet. "You're welcome."

O'Reilly propped himself up against the wall in a half-squat, hoarsely catching his breath. "I had him." He would have come up with something far more curmudgeonly were he not so preoccupied with restoring his blood-oxygen levels.

"You all right?"

"I'm fine. Help them!"

Dax nodded and left him to recover. Back to the fight. He located a discarded rifle on the ground and moved in, flanking Eyldwan and his last two henchmen standing. *Bang!* One down. Two down. Eyldwan didn't flinch. His eye was on the prize, the prize his enemies were currently attempting to dismantle in front of him. Several meters still stood between him and the pair of Alliance interlopers. The laser diode in his pistol had overheated, rendering it useless. He tossed it to the ground and searched for an alternative. Dax fired at him but missed as Eyldwan reached for his fallen comrade's rifle.

Dax lined up his next shot carefully and pulled the trigger again. *Click.* Empty.

He watched with dread as Eyldwan lifted the rifle, placing Logan in his sights. Dax was out of ammo and out of time. He did the only thing he could think to do.

As Eyldwan took the shot meant for the lieutenant's head, Dax hurled the rifle at him, striking him hard in the back and causing him to stumble. Eyldwan watched powerless as both weapons dropped through a large gap in the floor grating, landing in the subbasement far below.

"OH, EYYYYELIIIID!"

Dax figured the singsong taunt was a nice touch. Eyldwan turned to him, fury in his eyes.

"You."

"Me!" He continued on, cheerfully. Mockingly. "Oh, jeez, did I break your concentration? I'm really sorry about that. I just thought I should tell you something I've been feeling pretty guilty about. I kinda, sorta blew up your ship." Eyldwan glared at him. If looks could kill, his eyes would have launched nuclear strikes at Dax's feet. "Yeah, unfortunately I kinda wrecked mine, too, though. You got anyone else coming for ya? I could really use a ride."

"I should have killed you immediately."

"Yeah, should've. Didn't, though. Classic bad guy mistake. You know, there's a good example of that in *Commander Harrison* . . ." He snapped his fingers, trying to remember the film title. "*Commander Harrison vs the Belkinoids*! Didn't see that one? Ah, no worries. It wasn't the best of the bunch."

He kept it up, all the while with a cheeky grin on his face. The distraction was working. Logan and Sanders watched as Eyldwan slowly paced toward Dax, fist clenched hard enough to draw blood.

Sanders whispered to Logan. "What is he doing?"

"Keeping him busy. Come on, don't waste it." They continued ripping apart the connections.

With much of the distance now closed between them, the general and the commander stood facing each other. A tumbleweed may as well have rolled between them.

Eyldwan snarled. "I had hoped to give you a slow death. Let you watch your people enslaved, with their false idol powerless to save them. Now, I think I'd rather enjoy crushing your skull under my boot."

Dax's heart threatened to pound out of his chest. He wasn't prepared for the next thought in his head. That damned, awful, cornball line that he had delivered at countless prepared speeches, regaling the crowds with tales of phony victories and heroics. Suddenly, it was the singular thought in his head. As ironically appropriate as it was for the moment, it was all he could do not to laugh before the words escaped his lips.

"Earth? Surrender? Not on my watch."

Enough talk. Eyldwan charged at him like a mad rhinoceros. A new inescapable thought invaded Dax's brain. *This is gonna hurt.* And it did. Eyldwan sent him flying back several feet with a single massive blow.

On the bridge of the *Endeavor*, the ops station detected the impending descent of the warship remains. "Sir, the warship is drifting into the atmosphere! It'll be right on top of the colony in minutes."

Captain Nash took to the comms on an open channel. "*Endeavor* to Harrison! If you can hear me, you've got a dead ship incoming. Repeat, the sky is falling. Get your people out of there now!"

Dax struggled to return to his feet, crawling away, catching his breath, unable to answer. Eyldwan closed in, but Dax tossed a nearby box of tools at him, giving himself a chance to escape.

O'Reilly hobbled over to Logan and Sanders, the wound in his leg firing jolts of pain every step of the way. "You copy that, Weaver? We gotta get out of here!"

"We're not done yet!"

"It doesn't matter! This place is going to be a crater!"

"The pulse can still fire before then! Help us pull these cables!"

"Dammit!" He joined them, frantically ripping apart the jerry-rigged connections.

Dax and Eyldwan continued slugging it out. The general had strength and skill, and it was quickly made clear that Dax was severely outmatched. He spotted the large metal pipe from earlier and reached for it, but Eyldwan planted a knee in his face, sending Dax stumbling back. Landing on the floor, Dax noted a loose section of thick steel grating. Eyldwan pulled him back to his feet, eager to deliver another blow. Instead, Dax slammed the grating across his face. Eyldwan took a few disoriented steps back as Dax rapidly struck him again, across the face, then in the gut. Until Eyldwan caught Dax's arm and twisted it, forcing him to drop the grating. He followed up with a head butt, and Dax saw stars.

It was at that moment of pain and blurred vision that reminded Dax of a fight that escalated out of control some years earlier, and the secret weapon he had carried with him ever since.

He shook off his weariness, refocusing on Eyldwan. He unzipped the top of his jumpsuit enough to reach into his inner jacket pocket. Triumphantly, he produced the Darshyll liquor bottle.

Eyldwan stopped in his tracks. "Really?"

Dax surprised him with a stunning blow across his maw. Top-shelf, indeed. Dax had spoken the truth to Xihgat about his memento and the marital scuffle from which it originated. The high-priced liquor was supposedly some of the strongest stuff in the galaxy. What he failed to mention was that the limited-edition bottle itself was also made from one of the strongest metals known to the galaxy. It had worked on the furious husband, and it knocked a tooth straight out of Eyldwan's mouth.

While his opponent reeled, Dax took the moment for a quick celebratory swig, twisting the cap open with a long-awaited satisfaction. "Urrrmm!" He forced the gulp down with a shocked sour face. "Awck! That's awful!" He tossed the bottle aside immediately.

And so the fight went on. Dax used anything and everything available to him as a weapon, a distraction, or at the very least a nuisance to hold Eyldwan off. It was an epic battle between the seasoned soldier and the sloppy bar brawler taking cheap shots. Dax took an equally epic beating.

As Dax began to lose steam, Eyldwan slammed him to the ground. He could only lie there dazed as Eyldwan turned his attention back to the EMP. Dax spat the pooling blood out of his mouth and summoned every ounce of strength to get back up. He jumped on Eyldwan's back, attempting a choke hold, pulling him back into the fight. No matter what, he told himself, he would keep the general focused on him. This was the day Commander Harrison would do something truly selfless, the only way he knew how: getting his ass kicked.

The EMP device lit up, the whirring noise now at an almost deafening level. A beam of energy fired off from the satellite tower into space. On the *Endeavor*, systems overloaded and shorted out everywhere. The ship rumbled, and the crew rushed for cover from sparks and flame.

Outside the hub, Kiko watched in horror as bits of flaming wreckage began to hit the ground. She ran back into the shuttle as the engine began firing up. Dern sighed in relief, having finally managed to decipher a large portion of the controls. "Got it!" Kiko ran to him. "We gotta go!"

"No! We have to wait for them!"

Elydwan pinned Dax to the wall, lifting him off the ground in a one-handed choke hold. "So this is the best humanity has to offer? Ha!"

Dax managed a few hoarse words between gasps. "Not really. I've met better."

"Really? I know your world's history. Your people praise themselves for finally ceasing to slaughter each other, uniting under one banner to spread your *filth* across the stars. We were born in the stars. And you storm through, convinced of your grand purpose, your destiny granted by gods. Do you honestly put stake in such delusion?"

Dax's hand, grasping for anything, found Eyldwan's dagger sheathed at his belt. "Only when I'm buying lotto tickets." He stabbed into Eyldwan's side, sending him stumbling back and howling in pain. Dax saw the opening and rushed into him, tackling him to the ground. He laid into Eyldwan's face, punch after punch, bloodying his nose and mouth. He paused briefly, catching his breath, stunned at the turn of events. "I'm winning!" Eyldwan returned with a right cross from nowhere.

The energy pulse raged from the center of the control room. Logan, Sanders, and O'Reilly all converged on the final link to the satellite tower, an oversized heavy-duty cable. Logan wondered if they were already too late, but they had to try. "Don't stop!" It took all of their strength to slowly pull the connection loose, the magnetic effect of the device fighting them the entire way. Finally, it broke free. The cable came loose, and the energy beam ceased. The powerful whirring wound down as the device deactivated. Above them, the crew of the *Endeavor* watched with relief as the energy beam dissipated in space. The crew returned to their feet as the ship's systems began to restore.

There was no time for celebration. The facility rumbled as the wreckage storm outside worsened. O'Reilly helped Sanders to his feet. The strain had popped several of his stitches, and he was starting to bleed under his gear. "Time to go!"

Sanders looked to Dax and Eyldwan on the far side of the room, still struggling as the facility began falling to pieces around them. "Commander!"

Above, the satellite tower was battered with wreckage debris. The base creaked and strained, threatening to give under the increasing pressure. As Logan rushed to help Dax, the pylons started to give. The great tower leaned to the side, and a satellite detached completely, free-falling into the control room. Logan dove for safety. The giant dish obstructed the path, virtually cutting the room in two, blocking her from Dax and trapping him and Eyldwan inside. "DAX!"

Still grappling with Eyldwan, he shouted back over the ensuing cacophony. "Get out, Logan! Get to the shuttle now!"

"No!"

"Go, you idiot!"

O'Reilly and Sanders pulled her toward the exit.

The wreckage storm worsened rapidly. Kiko looked up from the shuttle's cargo ramp. The dead warship pierced through the clouds, burning in the atmosphere. Her eyes widened with terror.

The team rushed out toward the entrance, Logan and Sanders helping O'Reilly along as he powered through the pain in his leg.

Dern strapped into the pilot's seat. "That's it! We're leaving!"

Just then, Kiko spotted the team exiting the hub, debris falling everywhere around them. "Wait!"

Dern looked back from the cockpit. "For the love—move your asses!"

Kiko relayed at the top of her lungs. "Hey, you guys! Move your asses!"

They did. Logan called out as soon as they set foot on the ramp. "All in! Shut it and let's go!"

Everyone hung on as the ramp closed and the shuttle lifted off the ground.

Dax fell to the ground after a final blow from Eyldwan. Broken, bruised, bleeding. He had nothing left. Eyldwan looked around as his dreams of conquest crumbled before him. The satellite tower was toast. Exit blocked. The facility was coming down around them. There was nothing left for him now. He returned to Dax, pinning him to the ground with a heavy knee to the torso. Dax groaned.

"Very well. If I can't rid the galaxy of humans . . ." He wrapped his hand hard around Dax's throat. "At the very least, I will rid it of you."

Writhing on the ground as he ran out of air, Dax saw the warship coming down on them from above. It was all over now. Unless . . .

He activated the jumpsuit helmet control. The mechanical helmet rapidly protracted out from the neckline and clamped shut on Eyldwan's hand, slicing off several of his clawed fingers. Eyldwan reeled back, howling in pain, and Dax slammed a fist across his maw, knocking him away. Dax leapt to his feet and dove for the cover of the satellite dish. Eyldwan looked to the sky just in time to see a large chunk of ship landing on top of him.

He disappeared under the wreckage. The section of falling ship tore through the facility, dropping the flooring below into the lower levels. Chaos.

Outside, the shuttle continued speeding away. The crew witnessed the spectacular wreck in progress behind them through a small aft window. As the main bulk of the ship hit ground, it split into multiple sections. The ground quaked and the air was thick with a growing cloud of dirt, smoke, and flame.

They were not out of the woods yet. Before the shuttle could get far off the ground, a falling hunk of debris tore through one of the engine intakes. Alarms sounded off in the cockpit as Dern fought to stay in the air. "Shit! I gotta set it down!"

He fought long enough to put them at a safe distance, and they were soon landed in the dirt. Logan lowered the ramp and stepped out, staring back at the cataclysmic wreckage of the facility.

No way someone makes it out of that alive, she thought.

No way.

Not a chance.

She started walking anyway.

O'Reilly called out to her. "What are you doing? Weaver, there's no way."

She kept moving. Dern made his way out, inspecting the damage to the shuttle. "Don't worry, Doc. We're not going anywhere soon. That's for sure."

CHAPTER 17

CAPTAIN NASH SAT anxiously in his chair as the operations officer continued attempting to make contact. "Commander Harrison, are you there? Please respond. Crew of the SSV *Crichton*, do you copy? Any Alliance personnel, acknowledge." It was no use. The comms were dead. All static.

Logan arrived back at the hub after a long jog, burning out into a desperate walk. She took in the surroundings. A large portion of the satellite hub and surrounding colony lay in smoldering ruins. The landing platform and front entrance, though heavily battered, remained mostly intact. Whatever lingering hope she had that brought her there began to fade quickly. She let a moment pass, accepting it. She took a deep breath and thanked Dax in her head. The real Dax, not the commander known to the rest of the galaxy. She wondered, had he lived, if he might have eventually lived up to the legend. For his part, that day, she supposed he did, and she would see to it that the world knew that. But it was over now, and there was nothing left to do but turn back and head to the shuttle.

A sudden metallic scraping sound came from the entrance. Logan whipped around, sidearm drawn. Dax pushed a large hunk of burning sheet metal out of his way and exited the hub. Logan's jaw dropped. She walked to him slowly, meeting him on the landing platform. He limped toward her. He was broken, bruised, and bloody, his jumpsuit now half ripped off.

"How?" She thought she was shocked, but Dax's face showed an equal amount of disbelief. He stood nearly catatonic in his cluelessness.

"I got nothing. That dish was really sturdy, though. The floor, not so much." Most of it was a blur at the moment, but more details would return to him over the next few days. Diving under the satellite dish. Falling through the floor as the control room was ripped apart. Being thrown into the still-intact adjacent lower-level hallway, just barely out of reach of the growing crater of death and destruction.

For now, in his delirium, he simply looked to Logan. "How about you? You okay?"

She couldn't help but laugh, taking stock of his injuries. She nodded. "Yeah. Yeah, I'm good." She anchored his arm over her shoulders for support, and together they started the long walk back to the shuttle.

O'Reilly and Sanders sat on the cargo ramp, making fresh wraps for their wounds from Sanders's undershirt. Dern climbed out from under the wing of the craft, having cleared the last of the debris from the engine. He shook his head, mouth agape as he spotted the two approaching figures. "Unbelievable."

The doctor was naturally less impressed. "So he lives."

"Commander!" Sanders tried to jump to his feet and regretted it as he disturbed his stitches for the umpteenth time.

Dax mustered a grin. "Miss me much?"

"Dax!" Kiko ran in for a bear hug. Dax winced hard from his wounds, but the thought was still nice.

She looked up to him with concern. "Did you really blow up your ship?"

"Yeah, I did. I, uh, I was fresh out of rocks to throw at 'em."

"But what about SAMM?"

Oh right. He had almost forgotten. Dax hurriedly dug into his pocket, pulling out SAMM's CPU. He was not prepared for what he saw. "Son of a bitch."

Kiko feared the worst. "Is he damaged?"

"No! Not a scratch on him! The smug bastard." Dax talked directly at the piece of hardware, shaking it in the air. "You got off light!"

O'Reilly tightened the dressing on his leg with a grunt. "Well, I'm *very* happy the computer is intact, but it would have been nice if you'd been smart enough to take some *supplies* before abandoning ship!"

Dax rolled his eyes at the rant. "Doc—"

"My med kit was on there, you know. Now I'm shot; Sanders's stitches are opening. We'll probably all bleed out before the transports get here."

"Well, I'll bury you in the dirt right here! It'll be a lovely service!"

"Oh, shut up."

"You shut up."

Logan gave Dax a friendly pat on the shoulder to calm him, which merely caused him to wince again, bruised and broken everywhere. Several sonic booms rang out in the atmosphere, and the group looked up to see multiple Alliance cruisers finally arriving in the skies above.

Dax took a few wobbly steps forward, making sure he was clear of the shuttle. There in the open dusty terrain of Phobos, he raised his arm, painful as it was, and extended a defiant middle finger. "TWENTY MINUTES, MY ASS!"

The rest of the group joined him in the salute, as the evac shuttles descended upon them.

The usual inbound and outbound traffic had resumed around Central Station by the following day.

Nidahna, hands cuffed, was escorted across the security wing with a pair of officers closely behind. She would be transferred to a long-term holding cell while command sorted through the allegations. Bennett was present during the transfer, and her expression lifted as she saw him waiting for her.

"Xavier?"

The officers grabbed her to move her along, but the admiral waved them off. "Bila and Ranni are safe. It seems Utynai's men fled shortly after the battle. We have a team guarding your home while we track them down."

Nidahna breathed a sigh of relief. "Thank you."

"I also had it noted with the council that your actions were made under duress. Although, granting lenience will not be up to me." He spoke measuredly and did not look into her eyes. It was not an easy task to faze Admiral Xavier Bennett.

"Thank you. Xavier, I want you to know—"

"Good-bye, Nidahna." He continued down the corridor without looking back. Nidahna's eyes welled up as the officers moved her along.

A few hours later, Alliance personnel, civilians, and press gathered in the great hall. Logan, O'Reilly, and Sanders sat near the front of the audience. Sykes was also in attendance, standing in wait near the front. The hall was filled with chatter as a lone podium stood center stage, awaiting a speaker.

Finally, Dax and Bennett entered from a side door. The press immediately went to work, flooding the room with shouts for attention. Autonomous camera drones belonging to the assorted news networks rose into the air, competing for good angles as they hovered several feet above the crowd.

"Commander Harrison!"

"Dax Harrison!"

"We love you, Dax!"

"Commander, can you tell us what happened on Phobos?"

And so forth. As Dax moved toward the stage, Bennett stopped him for a whispered reminder. "Just the usual song and dance, all right? Nothing fancy out there."

Dax nodded and moved to the podium as Bennett joined Sykes, standing just off to the side of the stage. Instinctively, he snapped back into his public persona, waving to his adoring masses with a movie-star grin. There was only a momentary crack in the performance as he locked eyes with Logan in the crowd.

"Finally," O'Reilly groaned. "Let's get this farce over with and get out of here." He knew the score. The Alliance would sweep it all under the rug. They would spin the story by downplaying the danger of Eyldwan's threat, thus avoiding further panic and outcry. They would scrub any notion of an Alliance-built weapon and top-secret R&D lab. And Dax would once again fill the hero role, albeit in a more contained version of the events that in no way threatened Central Station or the entirety of Earth, for that matter.

The room hushed as Dax began. "Ladies and gentlemen, fellow esteemed officers. Today marks the tenth anniversary of the Allied Territories-Carteagan cease-fire."

He paused for the brief applause. "Ten years to the day of peace, but as you may have heard, we became dangerously close to that not being the case."

And you have no idea just how close, he thought. "You all know me and you know my story—"

Dax spotted Logan again, unable to look away. And with O'Reilly and Sanders next to her, his charming facade began to melt. It was time. It was time to end this. "And I'm here to tell you it's all bullshit."

There was an instant commotion from the crowd. He kept going, talking over it. "Most of what you've heard about me is a lie. I am not a hero." The noise in the room built and began to overtake him. "I can't . . . I . . ." He grew annoyed. He was trying to bare his soul, after all. "You wanna shut up a minute?! I'm trying to tell you something!"

Silence. Bennett made a move toward the stage, fuming. Sykes kept him at bay, immediately blocking him with an arm and shaking his head. He was right. It would only make things worse. The admiral relented, but shot Dax a look that spoke volumes. Quite probably, Dax assumed, volumes about wringing his neck. Logan hid a smirk.

"I'm no hero," he continued. "I actually hate that word. Well, I don't hate the word; I just hate being called it because that's not me."

Near the back of the hall, Kiko squeezed her way through the crowd to get a view. Dern stood behind her.

"But I have been lucky enough to be in the company of heroes. People like Lieutenant Logan Weaver, Corporal Alex Sanders, Med Chief Dan O'Reilly. Guys, you want to come up here?" He waved the crew up to the stage. They hesitated a moment, unsure what to do.

"Logan?"

She whispered back, shaking her head, "Dax, no."

Dax covered the podium microphone, leaning over to her. "Look, I'm already making an ass out of myself. Now, don't make it worse. Get up here!"

The crew made their way up. Dax spotted Kiko and Dern. "You guys too. Kiko, double-time it, buddy." Kiko excitedly bolted toward the stage. Dern gave Dax a polite thanks-but-no-thanks wave, and he acknowledged it with a small salute.

Logan, O'Reilly, and Sanders lined up on the stage, standing at attention as Dax carried on. "Some of the best and bravest officers"—huffing and puffing, Kiko finished her sprint to the stage—"and civilians I have ever had the privilege of knowing. They had my back out there, as well as all of yours. And I would certainly not be standing here if it weren't for them." He looked to them as he spoke. He wanted them to know he meant it. And they did. Even the doctor's usual grimace softened. "So, if you came here today for heroes, you're looking at them."

Dax held his breath for a few terrifying seconds, until the awkward silence shortly gave way to applause. He began to step away, relieved, as Bennett took the podium with an uneasy smile. He shook Dax's hand for the cameras while whispering in his ear, "This isn't over."

Dax smiled back. "You are absolutely right."

Before Bennett could react, Dax turned back to the microphone. "Excuse me, Ms. Chambers?"

A hand shot up in the middle of the sea of press. Marisa pushed her way through the crowd of journalists, making her way to the front. "Right here, Commander."

"Ladies and gentlemen, Admiral, I'm sure you're familiar with Ms. Chambers." He turned to her with a nod. "Marisa, always a pleasure. Did you happen to receive a package this morning?"

"I did, and made ten backups." Marisa revealed a holo-cell in her hand and activated it, holding it high for all to see. A loop of holographic footage began to play, and the hovering news drones swarmed for a closer look.

"Thank you, Ms. Chambers," Dax continued. "Before you ask, it's the footage of the Vega attack pulled from my ship's exterior cam logs. Courtesy of my SAMM unit."

Audible gasps and commotion stirred in the crowd as they watched the warship's assault on the memorial grounds, the destruction of the emergency transport, and so on. Dax let the images sink in a moment before he continued. "Yeah. Scary stuff, but important." He pointed to Eyldwan as the footage focused in on him and his ground crew. "See, there's Eyelid right there. I'm sure you all remember him. Not a happy guy. But wait, what's that?" He pointed to the EMP device as Marisa froze the footage on it.

Dax looked back at Bennett as he cheerfully continued. "Recognize that, Admiral? Kinda looks like an Alliance weapon-storage container. Wouldn't you say? Yes, it would appear to be your secret experimental EMP weapon, very clearly being stolen from the memorial grounds, or rather, your secret weapons lab built right under them. Wouldn't it?"

Bennett's eyes burned at him. "You arrogant prick."

"Yep." Dax wore it with pride. "Which would, in fact, violate the cease-fire treaty. Now, I'm not saying I'm an expert on the matter, but it would seem the Alliance has a bit of personal reflection to do if it's celebrating peace directly on top of some pretty illegal weapons of mass destruction."

The civilian and press crowds grew louder again, talking among themselves and demanding answers from the stage. Dax pushed on. "Now you all might be wondering why you should take *my* word for it, seeing as I just admitted to being not so honest in the past. Which is why I'm sure Ms. Chambers and her tech-heads at the paper can confirm the validity of the footage—"

"Already done," Marisa announced with a smile.

"She's a peach, isn't she?"

Bennett waved a demanding finger at Marisa. "That's enough! Shut it down, Chambers!"

"Not a chance, Admiral."

Bennett signaled a pair of security officers to secure Marisa
a   Dax, and the crowd went nuts. Marisa's press colleagues
r   de a human barrier, pulling her into safety behind them and
outing protests at her pursuers.

Logan held a hand to her head. "Oh, Dax." Meanwhile, O'Reilly laughed out loud at Bennett, and Sanders held Kiko ack from charging at the officers.

Dax continued addressing the crowd over the ensuing cacophony. "I've also provided Ms. Chambers with a full account on the fact-versus-fiction of my life, which you can read in her article soon." He kept going, shouting back as he was quite literally being dragged out of the hall. "Now I'm sure this might all be a bit confusing, and you may have a few questions for the admiral, so I'll leave you to it! Thank you for your time!"

Now this is more like it, Dax thought. The clean, spacious, and brightly lit holding cell was a definite step up from being bound to the wall of a Carteagan warship. He whistled merrily to pass the time, occasionally flicking at the energy shielding keeping him separated from the rest of the room. He had discovered, years earlier in a Martian drunk tank, that the Alliance shielding tech didn't sting or shock like the Darshyll-made equivalent. Rather, it merely produced a mild warming sensation, terrific for the back muscles if one were to lean against it just right.

After an hour or so, the holding cell door finally slid open, and Dax immediately recognized Sykes's disapproving voice. "You crazy bastard."

Dax remained in place, the warm shielding doing wonders for his sore shoulder. "Actually, sir, I believe I'm thinking clearly for the first time in . . . well, ever maybe."

Without warning, Sykes switched off the power from a wall panel, and Dax fell backward straight to the floor.

He complemented the heavy thud with a deep groan. "Ughhhh. That was unnecessary."

"Oh, you earned it, after that shit show."

Dax adjusted himself, sitting upright on the floor. "Oh, come on, that was funny. You cannot tell me you didn't love seeing that look on Bennett's face."

"A little," he admitted, as his stone-faced expression gave way to a grin. "Okay, a lot."

"What do you think the damage is going to be?"

Sykes pulled out his personal tablet, scrolling through the headlines. "If I had to guess, judging from the news so far, half the galaxy loves you. The other half might want to kill you."

"Ah. So, business as usual then."

"Not quite. You might have dragged Bennett down with you, but the council isn't going to take the public embarrassment lightly."

"Worth it. So, a court martial? Tar and feathering? Do they still do that kind of thing?"

"Now *that* I would pay good money to see." Sykes extended a hand and helped Dax to his feet. "Honestly, I have no idea what they'll do to you, but I'm pretty sure saving Earth and possibly all of the Territories might work in your favor."

Dax shrugged. "Here's hoping." Sykes turned to leave, but Dax continued. "Couldn't have done it without you, you know. Going over Bennett's head, sending the help. They owe you too."

Sykes turned around, waiting for the right answer.

"*I* owe you too. In fact, I've been meaning to ask you something."

Sykes held up a hand. "Harrison, I can put a good word in with the council, but I don't get to vote with them."

"No, no, not that. They . . . they put you in charge of me all those years ago. But you're not stupid. You knew who I was. You saw through the act. Why did you go along with all of it? Why go along with the lie?"

"Not my call."

"I know that. I mean, you're not Bennett. You're not the PR guy, and I don't see you as the type that takes bribe money. So why did you do it?"

Sykes looked him in the eye a moment. "Same reason a lot of us did. For the people."

Dax nodded.

"And," he continued almost begrudgingly, "I suppose I figured you had a shot to do some good with it. To make something of yourself, *really* make something of yourself. Didn't know it'd take ten damn years."

Dax chuckled. "Yeah, me either."

"Whatever happens now . . . today I'm proud of you."

"Thank you, sir." Dax was shocked, and touched. He saluted respectfully, before ruining the moment, as usual. "Wow, seriously though. Can I get all that in writing?"

"Never. You'll never hear it again. And if you breathe a word of this conversation to anyone, I'll recommend they space you."

"Jeez, what are you, friends with Eyelid? He wanted to fire me out the airlock too."

"Hm, guess you have that effect on people." An alert chime came from Sykes's tablet as a new headline scrolled across the screen. "Well, look at that. It seems the governor of Tarsis Three is recommending you for a knighthood."

"No kidding?" Dax's eyes widened. "I wonder what that would make me. Sir Harrison? Sir Commander? Sir Commander Dax Harrison, that's a bit much, isn't it? Well, maybe not commander after this."

"Sounds like you've got a few fans left after all." There was a knock at the door. "Speaking of that, you have visitors." Sykes unlocked the door, and Dax grinned at the faces he saw.

"Hey, guys!"

"Dax!" Kiko ran in first for the bear hug.

Sykes made a quiet exit as the rest of the crew filed in. Meanwhile, Kiko nearly choked the life out of Dax.

"All right, all right, easy. I'm not dying or anything. That was yesterday."

Sanders followed with a hearty handshake. "Commander, that was really great, what you said out there. Thanks."

"Hey, it was the least I could do for the real heroes of the Alliance, right?"

O'Reilly stepped in, appearing unamused as usual. "Harrison."

"Doc?" Dax prepared himself for the typical onslaught of insults. He was surprised as the doctor's face changed. O'Reilly paused briefly, as though he were mustering up the will to say something positive. He extended a hand instead, and they shook.

"You're still an ass."

"I know."

"Good." O'Reilly walked off with a satisfied smile, slapping him on the shoulder as he passed. His very wounded shoulder.

Dax forced a laugh back through gritted teeth. "Ah ha ha! That's still tender."

Finally, Logan came forward. "That was, um, a fine performance, Commander."

Dax sighed. "No performances, Logan. I meant every word."

"I know you did."

The inevitable occurred. A brief, awkward silence between them. Dax looked to Sanders, who took the hint and signaled Kiko to follow him out, giving them some space. Logan took notice and turned back to Dax with suspicious eyes.

"Um, I just wanted to say thanks. Really, thank you, for everything. . . . Also, if you do appreciate a good performance, I've been known to make an idiot of myself over a nice drink and/or dinner situation."

Logan tensed up. "Ah, you know, I don't think—"

"Just a friendly drink then."

She inhaled sharply, gritting her teeth. "Um . . ."

"A debriefing, in a large, public setting, with uncomfortable seats so you're never too relaxed."

With that, she laughed out loud, genuine and unguarded. She let him hang in suspense for another brief moment before she leaned to his ear. "It's a date."

Dax lit up. "Um, could you repeat that, please? Maybe speak up a bit? You know, a spaceship landed on me yesterday, and my hearing isn't too—"

She glared. "Don't push it."

"Right. Right, sorry."

She held a pointed finger to his chest, backing him toward the wall. Once he was across the shield line, she reactivated the barrier between them. "When you get out of here, one drink. A *friendly* drink, and you're buying."

Dax shrugged. "Sounds good to me, Lieutenant."

"Commander." Logan smiled and made her way to the door, calling back as she exited, "You better not be staring."

"I didn't—I wasn't—" The door slid shut as he muttered to himself. "Only a little." Alone, Dax leaned back against the shielding wall once again, pondering what would come next. Exposing a decade of lies, revealing classified operations, albeit illegal ones, and saving the world in one swoop. The council had its hands full. Depending on the decision, and how long it would take to come to one, he could be in there a good long while. He started whistling. At the moment, he really couldn't care less.

DAX HARRISON WILL RETURN. . .

THE GIRL IN THE VENTS

A SHORT STORY

CENTRAL STATION. 2175. (TEN YEARS BEFORE THE EVENTS OF *DAX HARRISON*)

LOGAN STARED INTO her breakfast, lost in thought until she smelled it starting to burn. "Damn!"

"Logan?"

"Don't worry, I got it!" She scraped the pancakes off the pan and onto her plate. Two of them were edible. The third she immediately dubbed a casualty of war and tossed it straight into the trash bin.

Johanna stood in her scrubs, wrapping her long hair into tightly wound buns. "That wouldn't be my lovely daughter burning down the apartment after I told her father how *responsible* she's been while he's away, would it?"

"Everything's fine, Mom. Relax."

Johanna chuckled, but her smile faded a moment later. Logan turned to see what caused it. They had left the Alliance News Network on the living room screen overnight.

"Unmute."

"—being told the number of casualties is currently estimated to be in the hundreds," the news anchor solemnly reported. Logan and Johanna starred on as footage of the aftermath played over the anchor's words. "With just as many injured or unaccounted for. Again, for those just joining us, the Martian settlement Sheparin was attacked by Carteagan forces in the early morning hours. Local Alliance patrols were eventually able to push the hostiles back, disabling several attack ships and forcing a retreat. However, nearly a third of the biosphere settlement has now been left in ruins."

"Oh my God."

Logan watched her mother's horrified expression, and it left a sickening feeling in the pit of her stomach. They both watched in silence a few moments as the coverage continued. The war always seemed so far away. Taking place in some other distant world. Quite literally, the Carteagan and Alliance forces had mostly remained entrenched in battlegrounds several worlds away. Now the conflict was knocking on their doorstep.

"They'll be sending some of them here. The biospheres can't handle those numbers."

Logan glanced to her mother again. She always admired her ability to stay so calm in any situation. How did she do that? Logan saw her mother break down precisely once, when Grandpa Frank died. But even now, with the Carteagan invaders inching closer, and Dad shipped out somewhere in the thick of it (where, exactly, they weren't allowed to know), Logan watched her mother simply shrug off the tragic news, take a deep breath, and continue preparing for the day ahead.

"It'll be a long shift," Johanna carried on, pinning a communicator to her sleeve. She pocketed her ID badge, grabbing it from the counter along with a banana as she neared the door. "Don't wait up for me, and please clean the kitchen when you're done."

"Okay." Logan remained fixated on the screen.

Johanna paused in the doorway with a "Hey," pulling her daughter back to the real world. "We're going to be all right."

Logan nodded, reassured.

"Love you, LoLo."

Logan rolled her eyes and mockingly replied, "Love you, JoJo!" The door slid closed, and the apartment grew quiet again, with nothing but the news continuing on low volume. Logan watched for another minute, then began feeling uneasy again. She changed the station. They were simply repeating the same information over and over now anyway. She switched over to a cartoon, hoping to distract herself, but it just felt dumb at the moment. Pointless. She shut the screen off and began contemplating what to do with the day.

She had an exam to study for. No chance of concentrating on that now. She finished her pancakes, which had gone a bit cold. She felt a brief pang of guilt about the casualty of war joke earlier, even if it was only a passing thought she had told herself. It still felt disrespectful.

The morning dragged on slowly as she made her way through the regular motions. She took a shower after breakfast (and made a mental note to clean the kitchen later), all the while drifting in and out of daydreams about Mars. She wasn't sure how she should be feeling. Every task just seemed to take a little longer than usual as her mind rampantly wandered. This became abundantly clear to her as the hot water abruptly switched to ice-cold, and she banged her knee on the shower door as she reflexively hopped away from the stream.

Fifteen minutes later she was dressed and still wandering aimlessly. She didn't want to turn the TV on again, but she found herself inevitably checking the feeds on her personal tablet. A few things managed to perk her up some. She scrolled through pictures of friends at a party last week, and watched a preview clip for the next episode of her favorite show.

It was when she opened the refrigerator (more out of boredom than actual hunger) that she began to imagine an attack on Central Station. The walls around her had always been home. An occasionally restrictive and boring home, but home nonetheless. Safe. Now Logan felt like those walls were slowly closing in on her. Or worse, she imagined them breaking away, destroyed by pulse blasts from Carteagan warships, pulling her helplessly into the cold vacuum of space.

She needed some air.

The sky above was a stunning bright blue, with only a few scattered clouds in the distance. Logan closed her eyes and breathed deep. Serene. It was all artificial, of course. A massive projection stretching across the hull above the promenade, meant to provide a sense of terrestrial normalcy. She knew this, but it still gave her the calm she needed. At least the station's square-mile park featured real grass and trees. She thought she might take the tram there later.

The moment of zen was swiftly interrupted by a crashing sound. Logan turned to witness a strange man struggling to his feet, cursing at the café table and chairs he'd just tripped over while simultaneously pulling himself back up with them. He kept moving, leaping over a public bench and ducking behind it. He peeked back over it briefly, then ducked again. He caught his breath, slowly. Finally, his head jerked to the side, spotting Logan, staring back from a mere five feet away.

Before she could think of something clever to say ("Who the hell are you and what are you running from?" for example), two more figures ran out from the path behind the café. Another human man and a Verdasian woman, both tall and dangerous-looking. They stopped as they entered the café area, scanning the promenade for their prey. Logan looked back to the crouching man, signaling her to keep quiet with a desperate finger held at his lips. She saw his eyes wild with fear, sweat beading on his brow. His clothes, disheveled. He was a complete stranger, but something inside told her she should help. It seemed like the decent thing to do.

She quickly pulled her personal tablet from her back pocket and pretended to fiddle around on it, slowly inching away from the hidden man. Nope. Nonchalant wasn't going to work. Logan heard their footsteps headed straight for her, but she fought the urge to look up and risk appearing even more suspicious.

"Girl!"

She casually looked up at the large beast of a man. "Huh?"

"Did you see someone run through here just now? Raggedy man in an overcoat."

"Umm." She shrugged and shook her head, being the best clueless teenager she could be.

"Knock it off, kid. He ran right out here."

Logan stared at the Verdasian woman. She had never met one in person before, let alone seen one so glamorous. Extensive tattoos ran along her blue/gray-tinted skin leading up to a neon-pink-dyed mohawk. She was the coolest alien Logan had ever seen. "Sorry, I wasn't looking."

"All right, enough playing around!" The man laid a large hand on Logan's shoulder. She protested immediately, pulling free.

"Okay! Okay! He went that way!"

The large man looked in the direction she pointed, far down the promenade toward a shopping center. "If you're toying with us," he growled.

"I'm not! I heard something, so I looked up and saw him running into the mall! Scrawny guy with a dirty coat, right?"

The Beast Man, as Logan began calling him in her mind, gazed down at her a moment, analyzing her. "Fine." He signaled his partner and began running toward the mall. The woman took a final look and nodded at Logan before following suit.

"Thanks, kid."

The hiding man peeked up again, cautiously watching as his pursuers disappeared into the maze of storefronts. Logan jumped as he suddenly shot to his feet.

"Hooo-ee! Thank you, darlin'. I owe you." He laughed, wiping the sweat from his brow.

"Um, sure. Guess I'll be going now."

"Whoa, now hold on there a sec, darlin'." He reached for her arm, and she snapped back.

"Hey! I'm not your *darlin'*. Just because I helped you doesn't mean I know you."

The man held his hands up apologetically. "Meant no offense, little miss. Just wanted to thank you proper for the help. I'm Ezekiel. Friends call me Zeke."

"Logan." He extended a hand and she shook it, but she kept a cautious eye toward him. "Who were those guys?"

"Some very bad people wanting to do some very bad things to me."

"And why's that?"

He hesitated, then reached for something in his coat pocket. "Well, Miss Logan, would you be up for doing me one more favor?" He held out a small rectangular stick. A holo-cell.

"Look, I don't know you, and I don't know what this is. I'm outta here."

"Come on."

She ignored him and kept walking.

"You'd be helping the Alliance!"

That got her attention. "What are you talking about?"

Ezekiel motioned to the viewscreens hovering above the café. "You hear what happened to the colonies?"

Logan nodded, the terrible news seeping back into her thoughts as the continuous coverage played.

"Makes you wanna do something, right? How about helping an Alliance officer complete his mission?"

Logan turned back to him, skepticism on her face. "*You're* Alliance?"

"Undercover. Tracking down smugglers. You know what they do? Make a sweet livin' off of sellin' weapons that make tragedies like that happen. And I need you to take this"—he placed the holo-cell in her hand—"and bring it to a secure location where my Alliance contact will be waiting."

"Why me? Why can't you take it?"

"My cover is blown, all right? Those two goons made me, and they've been on my tail all damn day. Now I might've ducked them for now, but if I get caught, it's best that thing is safe in someone else's hands. Someone they'd never suspect."

Logan fiddled with the device in her hands. Suddenly, she was feeling the weight of it. "I . . . I don't know."

"Ughhh!" Ezekiel punctuated his exasperation with rolling eyes and an obnoxiously loud groan. "Come on, kid! What are you, a Sterile Meryl?"

"Hey!" She punched him hard in the arm. "How about I just go find those guys again?!" She pointed threateningly at the shopping center.

"All right, I'm sorry, I'm sorry!" He put his hands up again in frantic apology. Logan meant business. Ezekiel kneeled down to her. "Look, you got heart, kid. I respect that. That's how I know you're right for the job. Whaddaya say? You wanna make a difference?"

Logan found herself continuing to habitually fiddle with the holo-cell in her hand, until she realized that probably wasn't a good idea and slipped it back into her pocket. She doubted anyone had seen her with it, but still, better safe than sorry.

Sterile Meryl, pshhh, she scoffed to herself. The slur, along with the male equivalent, Sterile Darryl, was directed toward stuffy Alliance types who lived and died on space stations like Central. The implication being that a lifetime subjected to CO_2-scrubbed air recycling and decontamination procedures at security checkpoints slowly rotted their brains. There was no basis for this, of course. The air was fine and fresh, and decon incidents were extremely rare. It was just a dumb insult, but it pissed Logan off.

"The drop is at Nolan's Lounge," he had told her. She had heard the name. A gentlemen's club on the far West End. Dad laughed to Mom about it once when a young private got in trouble with his new wife for being a frequent customer.

"I'm sixteen! They won't let me in there."

"Not inside. Just be out front of it."

Mom was right. The hospital was inundated beyond belief. Logan made her way through the halls toward Emergency Services. With the rooms filled, colonists lined the walls as nurses scrambled to triage as quickly as possible. She ducked her head into her shoulders as the cacophony of hacking coughs, moans, and outcries surrounded her. Still, she was unable to look away.

A nurse moving between patients bumped into her, and Logan found herself stumbling inches away from a man with a gaping head wound. She felt a sudden illness in the pit of her stomach.

"Logan!"

"Mom!" Logan rushed to her in relief.

"What are you doing here?"

"I—I just—"

"Come with me." Moments later, Johanna pulled her into a medical supply closet. The one area not currently in chaos, in which a private conversation was possible. She locked the door behind her and faced Logan, arms folded across her chest. "All right, young lady. What's going on? Shouldn't you be home, studying?"

"I know. I'm sorry. I just, I couldn't focus with everything going on and I . . . I want to help."

"Help?"

"Look, I know I've only been sixteen for, like, a day, but . . . it sucks."

Johanna shook her head. "I don't have time for this, honey."

"No, I mean it! It really sucks. I'm too old to pretend like all this stuff doesn't exist. And I'm too young for anyone to take me seriously and let me help. I just . . . I just feel like I should do something."

Logan probably would have felt worse about this manipulation if it weren't so rooted in truth. A truth she didn't fully realize until she vocalized it. Johanna's eyes softened to her daughter's plea.

"I'm sorry I left you in such a hurry this morning." She sighed. "I think it's great that you want to do something. I think your dad would be really proud of you. I am. And if you want to talk about this more later, we can, but I really have to get back to—"

"No," Logan started. "Could I, could I just, I dunno . . . grab some supplies for you or something?"

"That's not something I can . . ." Johanna paused, her eyes wandering as she thought to herself. "We do need more Synth-O-Neg."

Logan perked up. "What's that?"

"Are you serious about this? This is important. If I ask you to do something, this isn't something you can shrug off, like *studying*, for example."

"No, I mean it. Whatever you need." Logan nodded enthusiastically.

"West Medical Center. Talk to Dr. Schultz. Tell him I sent you to get as many units of synthetic O-negative as he can spare. Got it?"

"West Medical. Dr. Schultz. Synthetic O-negative."

"Good. Take my badge." Johanna unclipped her badge from her shirt and placed it in Logan's hand. She held on to her hand a moment, signaling her attention. "This is not official as far as Central Security is concerned. Use this to get on the tram and to show to Dr. Schultz, but keep it to yourself otherwise. Do you understand?"

Logan locked eyes with her mother and nodded. "I understand."

"Okay." Johanna smiled. "Try to be quick, okay? These people need help."

"Thanks." Logan felt a lump in her throat, only now realizing how much the moment meant to her.

"I gotta go." Johanna turned to the door and made her way out. "See you, LoLo."

"Bye." Logan stood alone in the supply closet. It was an odd feeling. Her plan had worked remarkably. The ID badge would allow her access on the tram to the far side of the station. She also had the opportunity to do some real good now, above and beyond Ezekiel's questionable mission that lay before her. Sixteen, perhaps, would not turn out as bad as she originally thought.

Logan stood in the center of the crowd of commuters. As everyone else stared at the hovering viewscreens above, she kept her eyes intently on her mother's ID badge in her hand. The tramway announced itself with a familiar suction of air reverberating across the platform. She watched as the tram cars slowed to a stop before her. She swiped the ID badge through the reader on the side of the tram car. She knew it would be accepted. Regardless, she felt herself tense up during the brief moment of processing. A moment later, she sat in a vacant seat as the car began to pull away from the station.

The minutes passed as Logan stared wide-eyed out the window. Central Station zoomed by at high speed. It wasn't often she got the chance to see it from this view. With classes, the mall, and most friends close by, there wasn't much reason to venture far from the East End. Besides, tram fare was twelve credits one way. What a rip.

The shoppers at Central Plaza gave way to a group of joggers on the walking path around the park, followed by glimpses of the lake, which Logan managed to catch between the trees. The fleeting bits of nature vanished as quickly as they arrived, and she shifted her gaze upward at the towering Embassies Building. She loved the sleek, dull-white look of it. Older people sometimes called it "ivory," which Logan learned referred to a long-extinct Earth animal. Gentle giants hunted to extinction. The facade wasn't constructed of *actual* ivory, but the thought came to her every time she saw it. A beautiful reminder of sad history.

"Cartaan trash."

Logan hadn't even noticed the pair of Carteagans at the back of the tram car. Like most refugees from Cartaan, they remained in hooded and modest clothing to avoid conflict while aboard the station. Conflict like the loudmouth human was currently attempting to stir up.

"Yeah, you heard me!" he shouted, despite their complete non-engagement. His dark green jumpsuit told Logan he was a maintenance worker. He stood closer to the pair, leaning into their faces until he could no longer be ignored. The male Carteagan calmly said something back to him. At least, it seemed calm. Logan didn't speak the language, but she could only assume it was something along the lines of "Leave us alone."

"You think anyone wants you here? I don't give a shit what the Alliance says. *Go home!*"

Logan counted at least seven or eight other passengers in the tram car, and no one said a word during the confrontation. Including herself. She felt a pang of shame as her mind raced, and she realized her own complex feelings on the situation. Mom and Dad made a point for her to know that not all Carteagans were the enemy. She even knew a Carteagan girl as a classmate last semester, and she never felt any malice from her. Still, it was difficult sometimes to separate the image of who her father fought against, who waged war against the Alliance, who caused so much destruction, from the innocents granted asylum on Central.

It was clear here and now, however, that the only malcontent present was a human one.

"Leave them alone." Her pulse raced as soon as the words left her mouth.

The bigot snapped his attention at her. He scoffed, "Bug lover," and casually turned back to his targets. "You understand me, croc-bug? You're not welcome here!"

It was at that moment the man stepped too close to the Carteagan's wife (at least, Logan believed her to be his wife, or girlfriend, or loved one of some sort). The Carteagan male rose from his seat and met the man face-to-face. A flurry of pent-up words spewed from the alien. Again, Logan didn't understand

Cardic, but the message seemed clear. The shouting continued from both men as the confrontation turned physical. The bigot attempted a collar grab, and the Carteagan swatted him away, hissing. The loud warning resulted in audible gasps from the other passengers. Logan watched carefully as the alien took notice and made the choice not to engage further. Instead, he lowered his hands and calmly stood between the harasser and his wife.

The man huffed, smugly. "Smart." But a moment after turning away, he turned back and shoved the Carteagan into the wall of the tram car. Nearly everyone jumped to their feet. Finally, the fellow occupants felt the need to intervene. Shouts of "Leave them alone!" "What's the matter with you?" and "You're not helping!" filled the car. One man exited to the adjoining car to find a security officer.

Logan saw an opening.

She ran toward the bigot and grabbed his arm hard, tugging him away from the refugees. "I said, *leave them alone!*" Without looking, the man knocked her away, and his palm landed across her face with a slap. Logan fell to the floor, and seeing the opportunity, immediately began to cry.

"Oh, Jesus, kid, I didn't mean—" Too late. The mob was turned in full force against the man. Several passengers swarmed him, pulling him away from the Carteagans and pinning him against the opposite side of the car, just as security arrived. An older woman came to Logan's aide, asking if she was all right and wiping her tears.

Logan kept up the act, but a brief moment transpired in which her eyes met with the now-handcuffed man. She made sure he saw her smile.

The tram car was deboarded at the next stop. In light of the incident, statements were required from all witnesses. Some complained about the delay. Others were quite eager to help. And as the commotion carried on out to the platform, Logan slipped away from the crowd, proudly inspecting the bigot's wallet she'd lifted during the struggle.

Serves him right, she thought. She pocketed the twenty credits inside, then found something even more intriguing. A Maintenance Level security card. If she could access the maintenance corridors below, it would allow her a path straight across the station. And since she was forced to get off the tram earlier than expected, it would certainly help shave some time off of her trek.

In her excitement at her new security clearance, Logan failed to notice the man directly in her walking path. She bumped into him hard, nearly stumbling to the ground. The man quickly caught her by the shoulder, helping her regain her balance.

"Whoa, slow down there."

She reactively prepared a snark-fueled "Watch it!" at her lips. Just before the words escaped, however, she noticed the uniform. Station security, and high ranking from the looks of the patch.

"Sorry."

He frowned down to her, but it didn't appear to be out of annoyance. He eyed her cheek, still freshly red from the slap. He also took notice of the crowd on the platform, from which she seemed to be hurrying away. "Everything all right here?"

Logan nodded, slyly pocketing the maintenance worker's badge still in her hand.

"What's your name?"

"Weaver, sir." She noted the name on his uniform, which read "SYKES."

"Weaver? Galen Weaver's kid?"

She nodded.

"Right, I know you." He smiled. "The Girl in the Vents."

Logan's face went warm, and both cheeks now matched in red. She knew exactly what he referred to: the stir she had caused with Central Security a few years earlier, adventuring through the ventilation system to see how far she could go. Really, it was an act of defiance from the family move to the station. She hadn't planned for it to get so out of hand. But when her foot got caught in some piping during one of her daily outings, she spent hours stuck and calling for help. As her parents came home to an empty apartment, they reported her missing, and a station-wide bulletin made her famous. The Girl in the Vents. Wow, ten years old felt like a lifetime ago.

"I hope you're not still trying your luck climbing through the walls."

"No, sir."

"Good, because the cleaning systems have been upgraded since then. It's dangerous."

She nodded again obediently, though she speculated whether it was actually true.

"All right, then." He took another look at the tram crowd. "Tell me, Weaver, what's that all about?"

Logan shrugged with a smile. "Just some crazy commuters."

"Hmm," was all Sykes replied with. *A very unconvinced "hmm" from the sound of it,* Logan thought. Yet, a moment later he followed up with a simple "Keep your nose clean, Weaver," and headed on his way.

"Yes, sir!" She called, perhaps a bit too enthusiastically. Her smile vanished as he called back once more.

"And keep away from the vents."

In an alcove near a mid-station food court stood a nondescript door to the maintenance level. Logan monitored from a counter seat at Tar D'syll Exotic Meat Palace. Needless to say, it wasn't an actual palace so much as a barbeque-style hole-in-the-wall. But the aroma was intoxicating as Logan realized she hadn't eaten since breakfast.

She moved closer, gulping down the last bite of skerzlobeast and tossing her skewer in the trash. No security camera, no guards around. The path looked free and clear. Naturally, the second she took a step forward, her illusions of an easy rest of the way came to a shattering end.

A familiarly powerful hand spun her completely around before she could react. Beast Man.

"Where do you think you're going, girl?"

He pulled her by her jacket sleeve until her back was against the wall. The Verdasian woman stood nearby, keeping an eye out for witnesses.

"Easy, Jurić! She's just a kid."

"Shut up, Rhea. I'm through with this running around." He leaned in close to Logan. "Now look, you, we see you sneaking around here and we know you're up to something. And our man Zeke wasn't anywhere near that mall. So you're gonna tell me what you know or, at the very least, where he is."

Logan tugged at her jacket, but it was no use. She couldn't break free. Beast Man Jurić shoved her back against the wall to make the point.

"Knock it off! You got nowhere to go. And don't even think of trying to scream for hel—"

She did. She screamed the mightiest scream she could muster, and it echoed fiercely through the corridor. Thrown off guard, Jurić's grip loosened ever so slightly as he scanned for any passersby who might have been alerted. It gave Logan just enough of an opening to plant her sneaker hard into his groin. He doubled over instantly, toppling onto his partner. Rhea cursed protests under his massive weight. Logan tried to run, but Jurić still held tightly to the jacket sleeve. She wriggled her way out and bolted to the maintenance door.

As the jacket came free, however, both Logan and Rhea witnessed the holo-cell fall out of the jacket pocket and onto the floor.

"The holo!"

"Grab it!" Jurić's words strained out of him between coughs and gasps.

"Get off me!"

As they continued to struggle, Logan swooped in for the device and dashed back to the door. She swiped the badge against the reader, too quick and frantic at first. A second try later, she heard the locks click open and rushed through the door, slamming it securely shut behind her just as her pursuers got to their feet.

It was a long but thankfully peaceful walk through the service tunnels. A labyrinth of pipes, junction boxes, water pumps, and other assorted things stretched on for what seemed like forever in each direction. Logan tried to make a game of guessing the purpose behind the various pieces of equipment. Mostly environmentals, air, heat, maybe sewage treatment. Actually, probably a lot of sewage treatment. Suddenly, she couldn't shake the thought. Just how many miles of pipe on this massive space station were dedicated to transporting—

Never mind, she thought. *I don't want to know.*

The guessing game dulled quickly. That was fine. Boring was welcome at the moment, as Logan felt things had become a bit too interesting today. And dangerous. Maybe this "mission," or whatever it was, was a mistake. Things were getting out of hand, and she wasn't entirely sure she was up to the task.

No. Stop it. She shook the thoughts out of her head. No more doubts. That was the whole point, to prove to everyone, including herself, that she *was* up to the task. To make a difference. No more games. No more silly little LoLo.

Of course, such a triumphant peace of mind was easier to maintain for those few minutes before Jurić and Rhea busted into the maintenance level.

Jurić announced their entrance with a shot that rang out through the service tunnel. Logan screamed as a ruptured O_2 cylinder hissed compressed air at her.

"You got nowhere to run now, girl! I want that holo!"

Logan ran as fast as she could, wondering how her pursuers had managed to find their way in. Not that it mattered. Jurić was right. There were no nearby exits and nowhere to hide in this part of the tunnel. All she could do was predictably run straight forward, sure to be caught in no time. She heard their boots growing louder, and her heart raced as she forced her legs to move faster, her lungs to work harder. *Where the hell are the exits?!*

Finally, a door! She had made enough distance to give it a shot. She swiped her stolen badge, and a negative chime rang from the panel. She swiped again to no avail, then saw the "Security Level 4" indicator above the panel. The badge read "Lvl 3."

"Shit!" She kept running, but she was already exhausted and losing steam fast.

"Come on, kid," Rhea called. "We don't wanna hurt you—"

"Speak for yourself," Jurić grumbled.

"*I* don't want to hurt you, but no more playing around! Just give us the holo-cell and you can run on home!"

Logan tucked herself behind a column of oversized pipes, pressing as flat against the wall as she could. She did her best to quiet her huffs for air. It was a temporary hiding spot at best, but she hoped the low lighting of the tunnel would work in her favor. Then Rhea flicked on a flashlight, dashing said hopes.

I'm dead. I'm so dead. What the hell was I thinking? This is stupid. I'm so stupid.

As Logan began to tear up in her panic, she noticed a ventilation grating on the far wall.

Keep away from the vents. Sykes's warning didn't matter now. What could be more dangerous than certain death at the hands of the rapidly approaching Beast Man? She would have to run directly across the hall to the vent, right in the path of Rhea's flashlight beam. No other option now. She flung herself across, fingers outstretched to instantly begin tugging at the grating.

"There!"

Jurić unsheathed a shock blade from his belt, the pop of sparks echoing through the tunnel. Rhea closed in. But as she rounded the corner, the flashlight shone only on a discarded grating and an open vent above it. As Jurić caught up and saw the same, he slammed a fist down in the vent with a grunt.

"Dammit."

Logan scooted along the vents. There was no telling what direction she was headed, but it was away from Jurić, and that was all that mattered. Pitch-black darkness enveloped her as she moved past any light source. The space felt much more cramped than she had remembered, and it kept her on edge. Hardly enough space to even crawl on hands and knees. It then dawned on her that she was much smaller the last time she'd done this.

Again, she conceded that anything was better than her previous situation. Even if she ended up backtracking a bit, wherever she exited, she'd take the rest of the journey in a more public setting. If there was any chance of running into trouble again, better it be out in the open than stuck down here. At least the vents weren't all that terrible, save for the lack of comfortable space. It was even becoming clear now that those supposed "dangerous upgrades" were all talk. Sykes's way of keeping her out of trouble. *Valiant effort, sir.*

Then she heard the humming.

It started small, in the distance. Some sort of hum or buzzing sound, accompanied by a periodic click. Electrical maybe? Logan scooted farther down and realized she was able to see her hands. Just barely, but there they were, in dim red light. The light grew stronger the closer she came to a junction. She arrived and turned to see a sustained laser grid, clicking as the emitters rotated the pattern. This combined with an integrated germicidal UV light would deny passage to germs, pests, or Logans of any kind.

Okay, maybe he wasn't lying. She *very* carefully shimmied the rest of her body past the junction and away from the light parade of doom. *Nothing to worry about,* she mentally reassured herself to little success. *Just need to be careful and I'll be fine.*

Another series of clicks began, faster this time, and the light grid began advancing toward her.

"*Nooo!*" She moved. She moved fast in a wild panic. The grid moved slowly, but it was coming for her, without a doubt. Programmed to detect motion or contagions, perhaps. She didn't stick around to ask it. She looked ahead and saw another junction down the shaft. She scrambled for it, hoping to find an exit around the corner. A grate, an opening to the plaza, somewhere with people she could call for help. As she approached, however, she was met with another red glow.

She screamed. She screamed and pounded at all sides. "*Heelllllp!*"

After a moment she noticed this grid fixture was not giving chase. It made the familiar clicking sounds, but refused to budge. Logan listened closer to what sounded like a busted gear straining inside one of the laser emitters. As she shifted her weight, she felt a sharp pain in her butt cheek. She screamed in terror, assuming the pursuing grid had caught her. It was in fact the stolen maintenance badge poking from inside her back pocket. She had a wild idea. The outer layer of the badge was a hard plastic, but she knew there were some sort of metal parts inside. There had to be, right? Maybe she could reflect the laser with the layer of metal inside the badge, and burn herself an exit. She was pretty sure she had seen something like that in movies. It was worth a shot.

Please don't burn my face off. Please don't burn my face off.

It didn't, but it melted the badge with ease. There went that plan. *Mirrors,* she realized. It was mirrors that reflected lasers. Shit. She suddenly wished she was one of those makeup-wearing girls that kept small mirrors with them at all times.

She then noticed the broken emitter not only refused to move but also appeared to be coming loose from the rest of the fixture.

Please don't burn my fingers off. Please don't burn my fingers off.

She carefully gripped the sides of the emitter and tugged at it. It didn't budge. She heard the clicking of the pursuing fixture growing louder from behind. She tugged harder, careful not to let her sweaty fingers accidentally slip into the path of the laser. The emitter wriggled slightly looser. Just enough to manipulate the direction of the beam. Logan gasped with relief, then in horror as she saw the pursuing lights drawing near.

At that very moment, Urib'han Toktavnon, son of Ot'ud Toktavnon, ambassador of Dusmiri V, and self-proclaimed bona fide ladies' man, smeared a glob of mustache wax across his whiskers. His meticulous ritual was narrowed down to a science, and he took calculated use of the styling gels, colognes, and so forth laid out at the vanity mirror. The delicate external mucus membranes of his species didn't always make human grooming customs easy for a Dusmel such as himself, and he took pride in his finely tuned skills. His lady guest awaited entertaining in the lounge area of the suite, when a series of strange noises began emanating from the ceiling. *Thump. Thump. Thump.*

"Urib?"

"Just a moment, my pet."

A sharper metallic banging followed, and Urib'han backed away slowly from the vanity. A red-hot laser pierced through from above. Urib'han screamed and dropped his cologne bottle as a sixteen-year-old girl fell to the ground in a flurry of chaos and ceiling fragments.

"Did I or did I not say the vents are dangerous?"

. . .

"Well?"

"You did," Logan meekly replied. She sat with her head low, avoiding eye contact as Sykes fired his reprimands across his desk at her.

"You want to tell me what the hell you were doing in there then? And why I have a Dusmel ambassador raising hell about the new sunroof in his private quarters?"

"Iwasbeingchasedbythesecrazygangstersorhitmenor somethingthatwantedtokillmebecauseIhadsomething theywantedandIwasjusttryingtohelptheAlliancebutthen theycameaftermeandstartedshootingatmesoIwentinto theventstogetawayand—!"

As the crazed, one-breath, rapid-fire explanation carried on, Sykes rubbed his temple and remembered why he didn't have children. "All right, all right, *hold it!*"

She did.

"Slowly. From the beginning. In detail. All of it."

She nodded, and laid it all out. Zeke, her mother, Beast Man Jurić, Rhea, who was at least kinda cool but definitely also one of the bad guys, the jerk from maintenance, everything. She thought of the trouble she was likely in, and how she would be disappointing her mother, and her words started to choke in her throat. "I'm sorry. I just wanted to help."

Sykes said nothing, but Logan got the impression he was deciding what to do with her. Would he arrest a minor? She did steal a badge. And entered an unauthorized area. And destroyed an apparently important guy's ceiling. And here she wanted to be taken seriously. She supposed serious punishment came along with it.

"Is this your guy?" Sykes slid a tablet across the desk. On the display was an image of Zeke, looking more clean-cut than Logan last saw him. Probably from his official Alliance record, she assumed. She confirmed with a nod.

"Hmm." With that, he rose from his seat, pulled the holo-cell (which he had confiscated) from his pocket, and tossed it back to her. "Well, let's get a move on."

"Where?"

"To complete your mission."

The facade of Nolan's Lounge was decidedly subtle, though a peek through the entryway assured that the interior was anything but. Logan believed she saw some kind of fur covering the walls as a patron made his exit. She needed only pace outside for a few seconds before a familiar disheveled coat fluttered her way.

"Sweet Jesus, girl. It's about time!" Zeke removed his disguise as he approached. His disguise was comprised of cheap plastic sunglasses and a baseball cap with "I LOVE NOLAN'S" embroidered on the front. (Though, in place of the word "LOVE" was actually an upside-down heart symbol.)

Logan held up the holo-cell but pulled back as Zeke immediately attempted to snatch it from her. "Come on, no games, darlin'. Give it here."

"What are you doing here? I thought I was supposed to be meeting your contact."

Zeke shrugged. "Don't worry about it. The important thing is you're here. Now let me see the thing."

"Hey! I almost died because of this, you know."

"And the Alliance thanks you for your service. Fork it over."

"Yes, the Alliance does." Sykes strolled out from the corner of the building, and Zeke's face dropped.

"Aww, nuts." He made a short-lived dash in the opposite direction, where he was immediately met by two security officers with cuffs at the ready. Sykes greeted him with a smile.

"Ezekiel Lutz, I am incredibly not surprised."

Zeke rolled his eyes at him. "Something I can do for you, sir? I'm kinda in the middle of something with my friend here."

"Yes, I see that." Sykes held the holo-cell to his face. "Half-assed smuggling is one thing, but using a kid to get your merch across station? Putting her in your buyer's line of fire? You're hitting some new lows."

"The deal may perhaps have gone a bit south."

"Trying to scam the highest bidders with your outdated access codes? I can't imagine why they'd be upset."

Zeke's eyes widened. "Outdated?"

"Of course, you fool. Did you even look at what you stole?"

"Hang on." Logan couldn't keep quiet any longer. "So, he's not Alliance, is he?"

"Was," Sykes corrected. "Some time back. Couldn't cut it, could you, Lutz?"

"Not all of us are made for the rank and file." Zeke put his chin up at Sykes. "Stand at attention, follow orders, ask no questions? Maybe I just wanted more outta life. Doesn't make me a bad guy. Does it, darlin'?"

Logan's brow furrowed at him. For one, she had enough *darlin* for the day. Also, she wasn't buying into any more of Zeke's schemes. "And these access codes. What do they access?"

Sykes paused a moment. "Munitions stores. Weapons that could have been stolen and used against the Alliance and civilians."

With that, Logan kicked Zeke full force in the shin. He groaned, sinking to the ground, save for the security officers holding him up by the arms, and Sykes held Logan back from further blows.

"All right, get him out of here." They did so, and Sykes brought Logan over to a public bench to sit as she collected herself.

"He made me think I was helping!" she shouted. Her face was red, and she fought back tears, replacing them with anger. "He said I could stop things like what happened on Mars."

Sykes was noticeably uncomfortable around the crying child, but he placed a friendly hand on her shoulder. "Well, if it's any consolation, you *did* help. We got Lutz, thanks to you, and we're tracking down the other two as we speak. They won't get far."

Logan perked up a little. She supposed, in an unexpected way, she had managed to help keep Zeke and his buyers from causing any more trouble. *Trouble,* she thought.

"Am . . . am I still in trouble?"

"Oh yes," Sykes answered without hesitation. "No question. Trouble you are in."

Logan's head sank again.

"But we'll get to that later. For now, I think I've held you up enough. If I recall, you've got another mission to finish. Isn't that right?"

Mom. The hospital. The synthetic blood. She had almost forgotten. "Right!" She shot up from her seat. "Umm . . ." She looked to him for permission.

"Go." He waved her off. "Get a move on."

She did, and ran off like a shot.

"And if they give you any grief at West Med, tell them I authorized it. They can talk to me."

"Got it," she called back.

"And take the tram! Not the vents!"

The evening hours back home came and went. Logan lay on the living room couch, zoning out of the world as she tossed a baseball in the air above her. There was still no chance she was studying for her exam.

She thought about the day. A flare of anger rose in her as she thought of Ezekiel. But it softened as she thought of Mars. And the survivors at the hospital. And the proud look on her mother's face when she delivered the blood as promised. She did express some concern, however, as apparently Sykes had already reached out about "a discussion that needed to be had" about her daughter.

Logan still had the apartment to herself as Johanna finished the last few hours of a very long shift. She cleaned the kitchen, finally, and tidied up the place in general. She knew her mother would see through it, but Logan was prepared to suck up anyway. In the event Johanna did have that talk with Sykes, and came home with steam coming out of her ears, Logan would be the model daughter. She would have cooked a late dinner, but admittedly her cooking skills didn't extend much further than half-burned pancakes.

When Johanna finally walked in, she simply joined her daughter on the couch, gently pulling Logan's legs out of the way and sitting on the far end.

"Hi."

"Shhh." Johanna sighed with her eyes closed. "Just want to rest for a minute."

"Okay." Logan smiled and began casually getting up from the couch.

"Why did I get a call from Central Security today?"

She reversed back into her seat. "Umm . . ."

"Logan."

She shrugged. "I think they can probably explain it better than I can."

Johanna gave her the eyes. The knowing mom eyes. "I think you can explain it just fine, but in the morning. Right now, you're going to tune the screen to the long-range."

Logan's gasped, her face lit up with joy. "Dad?!"

"He should be on in about ten minutes."

Logan spent the next minutes eagerly sitting just a few feet away from the living room screen. She stared at the static, not wanting to miss a second of the incoming transmission. Johanna poured a glass of water and continued relaxing on the couch. When the connection finally came through, the typical enthusiastic "hellos" and "I love yous" were exchanged.

"Happy belated birthday, Lo!" Galen announced it so his fellow crewmen could hear, and Logan and Johanna laughed as scattered cheers could be heard from the background. "So how does sixteen feel?"

Logan suddenly wanted to tell him everything. Even the parts that would get her in trouble. Instead, she simply shrugged with a smile. "Eh, it's all right."

ABOUT THE AUTHOR

TONY VALDEZ is a nerd, podcaster, musician, writer, and a skilled producer of silly faces. He also loves great stories found in books, comics, film, TV, video games and so on. He was born and raised in San Diego, California and currently resides in Orange County with his lovely wife. He misses home, but Disneyland is nice.

GRAND PATRONS

AJ Sevilla
Ashlee Hall
Ava Pasco
Diana Valdez
Dria Parra-Diaz
Jordie Henderson
Kristin Naomi Garcia
Leticia Valdez
Lyndsay Anne Winkley
Michael Marshall
Max Armani
Meg Valdez
Rachel Trujillo
Ricardo A. Henriquez
Ryan Phillips
Todd Cummings
Kathy Davies
William Bennett Jr
Rita Bareno
Sandra Valdez

INKSHARES

INKSHARES is a reader-driven publisher and producer based in Oakland, California. Our books are selected not by a group of editors, but by readers worldwide.

While we've published books by established writers like *Big Fish* author Daniel Wallace and *Star Wars: Rogue One* scribe Gary Whitta, our aim remains surfacing and developing the new author voices of tomorrow.

Previously unknown Inkshares authors have received starred reviews and been featured in the *New York Times*. Their books are on the front tables of Barnes & Noble and hundreds of independents nationwide, and many have been licensed by publishers in other major markets. They are also being adapted by Oscar-winning screenwriters at the biggest studios and networks.

Interested in making your own story a reality? Visit Inkshares.com to start your own project or find other great books.